MYSTERIES AND STRANGE EVENTS

by

Drew Jones

DEDICATION

...For all my family, thanks to T & R,

and apologies to Monty, who has had to wait a

little longer for his walks.......

.

CONTENTS

THE RETURNING 4.2

"Classic cars...those obsolete machines that in their day were the pride and envy of many, and when their day was over were promptly exchanged or scrapped at their owner's whim...many simply left to fade. We've all seen these old matriarchs of yesteryear on today's choked roads and given them a second glance as we continue on our journey, some exit the stage gracefully while others refuse to rust away."

One muggy late August night in 2015, Terry Daniels left or rather staggered from his local The Six Bells, and groped his way homeward – a distance of two miles. The Six Bells was nestled deep in Oxfordshire's finest postcard countryside and little stirred that night as Terry finally reached the main road. He would follow this for a mile to reach his village and not long after that his front door.

He stopped his clumsy journey after 10 minutes and propped himself on a five-bar gate and was now experiencing that "I wish I hadn't had that last one" moment when all at once he heard a car approaching from the direction he had travelled. A mist was forming close to the road surface and the sound of the vehicle approaching shattered the stillness well before the vehicle was close.

Terry leaned back on the gate and became an avid spectator as this late arrival showed itself. "An old Jag!" he thought in amazement. Sure enough, a large Jaguar Saloon thundered into sight. Terry's late father had owned one and he recognised it at once even taking into account his current condition courtesy of The Six Bells hospitality. The familiar grill and blazing round headlights met his gaze and were replaced by the sleek boot and twin exhausts. This he was sure was a series 3 XJ6 and the familiar sound had to be a 4.2 with the legendary XK straight six engine.

The old car carried on past him at tremendous speed and then the driver slammed on the brakes and probably with the aid of the handbrake, the huge machine with much tyre roar and smoke, half spun half skidded across the road and into a lay-by on the right-hand side of the road. It was a long lay-by as it had once been the old road before the current main road had been built. The Jag continued up half its length and suddenly stopped…and then silence.

The disturbed dust began to settle, and under the clear skies, Terry moved forward from his observation point to study the car which was bathed white in the moonlight. It had come to a halt under some trees and he was unable to make out a driver due to the dark shadows from the branches. Moving closer still he confirmed it was indeed a series 3 XJ6 and what he thought was dark brown in colour with stainless steel wheel trims. Part of the number plate was something, something 313X - it looked like an early one. He was baffled why the owner of this lovely old car would be out so late and thrashing the poor aging beast. Could it have been stolen?

Just then the sound of the starter motor startled him and the car rocked as the straight six bursts into life. The long sleek body snaked as the rear wheels struggled for traction on the loose road surface and then found the tarmac. Terry felt its fury as it destroyed the distance between them and passed him on the side of the road. He could feel heat from the engine touch his face mixed with a scent of oil and then exhaust fumes.

He again was left to watch the boot, distinctive rear brake lights and twin pipes, as the old Jag sped away from the scene back the way it had appeared, the lights getting smaller and smaller until swallowed by the growing ground mist.... then silence returned.

The identification of this late-night prowling car was correct, it was a Jaguar series 3 XJ6 4.2 fuel injection straight six with 3 speed automatic gear box built in 1982. First registered in Oxford, metallic brown in colour and fitted from new with suede seats (not leather) which was unusual, maybe on special request. As with all old jags it had a lovely fitted wooden dash and gauges made by Smiths. And never forgetting the comfy armchairs and all-round gentleman's club feel. These cars in their day were really elegant cruisers... I digress.

The first two years of its life were spent registered to a large engineering company and like so many big Jags it spent it's time with this firm running company directors to and from meetings, pounding motorways and was also a frequent visitor to the large well-known airports.

In early 1985 this still much desirable machine was sold off privately to a Mr Potts from Wiltshire. This was and is common practice with big companies – all fleet cars have an allotted time.

Potts was an accountant in his late 50's and as my father would say "looked like a rasher of wind." He was a timid man, never argued a point, never cut in line in the refectory to get a better seat and never really seemed to enjoy life. When asked to the annual Christmas party he would always give the reply - that attending would give him indigestion.

Potts did have a saving grace. It was the recent and

totally out of character purchase of the already mentioned Jaguar XJ6. He lived alone and had always fancied owning such a car. And in case you're thinking his meek personality mirrored his driving abilities you'd be wrong. He could turn the XJ6 on a sixpence and was often seen belting down the fast lane on many a motorway. Once out of the car he seemed to deflate and shrink from people.

Into Mr Potts's life came his new boss, a Mrs Webb whose sole purpose during her working hours seemed to be to make Potts the butt of all office jokes and generally see that his life at work was as unhappy as possible. If the books didn't tally, if the stationery went missing, if the coffee machine had broken etc etc it was always suggested that Mr Potts was to blame.

She was a chubby overbearing woman with florid cheeks, a short black crop of bushy hair that could have been carved out of her head, a penchant for loud dresses which always showed her bloated ankles to an alarming extent. Maybe she identified Potts as the obvious weak target or maybe it was because he had applied for the job she now occupied and abused, but whatever the reason, Potts was made to suffer.

As the months rolled by under the tyranny of Mrs Webb, Potts's resolve began to buckle and on more than one occasion he would pull up at work in the gleaming XJ6 only to find himself under her jealous gaze from the window. He would sit in the sumptuous interior until the last possible moment before going in to face the abuse. He had also taken to having his lunch in the XJ6.

One afternoon in particular Mrs Webb came in late and in front of the whole office announced that Potts's car was responsible for damaging hers. He protested strongly to which she said that his car was far too big for such little spaces, it hung over the allotted space marked, and was to blame for the damage to her vehicle.

The next morning it seemed that even the XJ6 had turned on him. The old girl stubbornly refused to start and as the time ticked by, he became more and more worried...Webb! This would be her latest weapon to use against him. At last the engine woke up and he hurried the big old barge to work. Because of his late arrival, he would have to park further down the car park out of sight of the windows overlooking his usual space.

Mrs Webb must have been delighted by his late arrival - her florid flabby face was trying to show anger but she was really beaming. After another public dressing down, he was told he would now have to use his lunch break to catch up and that would mean no sneaking out to his car to hide.

... Mrs Webb's funeral was a lurid affair with tawdry flower arrangements adorning a pink coffin.

The police had questioned Potts a few hours after her death amid growing alarm in the office and speculation. The police had explained it to Potts thus wise. Webb had left the office at 1pm to visit the high street for lunch as normal and not long after had been killed outright after being hit by a vehicle. Potts asked the obvious question why was he being questioned?

Several people had come forward with information that prior to the accident, a large Jaguar saloon matching the one owned by him was seen in the area and had even been observed close behind Mrs Webb - almost as if following her...

Potts retorted and made the statement; was he being told his car hit Mrs Webb?

What actually had happened was that the driver of this Jaguar had blocked Mrs Webb from the view of an oncoming bus. The Jaguar had then swerved at the same time as blowing its horn. The result was to startle Mrs Webb who then blundered into the road, the bus turned sharply to avoid the large saloon but had not seen the pedestrian. The Jag then floored it and left Mrs Webb to take her chances, but even her ample frame could do little to fend off a large bus. The mess was considerable.

Potts of course was soon cleared of any wrongdoing as he hadn't left the office and most of the staff could vouch for him. The immaculate XJ6 was checked over, but there was no evidence of it having been stolen. Because on the day in question, the car had oddly refused to start that morning and had caused him to be late, forcing him to park at the rear of the car park where no one could tell if it had gone missing at any time. Had he assumed his usual space then the car's absence would have been noticed definitely...

Mr Potts reluctantly said goodbye to his old friend in 1989 after suffering what doctors called a life changing huge stroke. The solicitor arranged the sale of the car along with his house to pay for a warden controlled flat with private care. The last time he ever saw of the car, it was gleaming under its car port waiting for its next turn of duty.

. . . .

The downfall of Mr Kemp, the next owner of the XJ6, can really only be laid at his own feet and is fully deserved…although how the damning evidence which brought about his incarceration was delivered will long baffle him.

Kemp was in his mid-thirties and was to all intense and purposes - a con man. He picked the car up through an auction in late 1989 or early 1990. By then the Series 3 had been replaced by a newer model and was already feeling outdated.

Kemp was in property development and he often took the car all-round the UK. It received maintenance only when absolutely necessary. It was tarted up if he was trying to impress his next client, but other than that it had assumed a grubby appearance that even the impressive lines found hard to conceal.

On many occasions the Jaguar would be made to work all night as Kemp drove from his flat in Reading to possible clients and back again. The tried and tested engine effortlessly transporting him further and further with little in the way of gratitude in return. As the speeding fines for the XJ6 grew Kemp's luck seem to dwindle. With a final roll of the dice he and a colleague got involved in a holiday development scandal.

In its most basic terms, the idea was to get people interested in acquiring land in Spain and having a luxury villa built. They would be taken out to see the land and if happy a deposit of £10,000 was handed over. When a minimum of 30 victims were onboard it would then be announced that the company had gone bust and these unfortunates would be left trying to fight a legal battle in Spain while, Kemp and his associate channelled the money elsewhere. To convince his potential clients of his credentials, Kemp embellished heavily from a genuine and legitimate real estate company in London where he had worked previously - even down to using their headed paper and business address.

With the con almost complete Kemp travelled to London with his passport and the falsified paperwork relating to the swindle, to meet his associate to discuss their "disappearance" plans. He stopped at a service station to get something to eat and make a call to his anxious partner.

Kemp informed his collaborator that he would be with him in an hour... then a few yes and no's followed, then a pause. He looked back at the melancholy car with its side lights staring back at him and stated that it could be dropped off at a breakers yard he knew before they left London. The Jaguar was behind him as they spoke, sadly the low sleek body was covered in mud, the chrome grill spotted with insects and the stainless-steel wheel trims filthy black from brake dust.

A few seconds later a bus pulled into the carpark and came between him and the Jaguar, several people got off and there was a hubbub and hustle as people retrieved their luggage. Kemp finished his call and was at once startled to see the XJ6 pulling out of the services and heading for the motorway access slip road!

He sprinted towards the dirty brown dowager as it neared the acceleration lane, he couldn't make out who was driving in the dusk sky and dirt covered the rear window. He must catch up with it if only to retrieve his papers…! The XJ6 negotiated a mini roundabout, and then the bonnet lifted as whoever was driving floored the big car and the huge engine sprang into life and put down over 200 horses through its automatic gear box. Within seconds it was headed towards London and out of sight.

Mr Kemp and his colleague both received 6 years imprisonment for masterminding a foreign property swindle with the sole purpose of defrauding people. It was pointed out that this was not even an honest venture gone bad as it was purely a con from its conception. The investors' money was retrieved and the judge in his deliberations also highlighted a particularly fascinating, if somewhat dubious lucky break that had uncovered the deception.

Kemp's car had been found with its front passenger door open and engine neatly idling parked in the managing director's parking space of the well-known London real estate company that Kemp had had connections with in the past. Documents were discovered strewn on the passenger seat bearing the company's logo and so were taken inside for safe keeping until the car's owner could be traced. The

Judge let out a snort and expressed his opinion that it was highly likely a disgruntled colleague in on the swindle had dropped the car off to expose the scam as revenge for some kind of double cross.

· · · · · · · ·

Not much is known about our aging XJ6 throughout the 90s. It was purchased in 1996 by a man only known as "Gary". By this time, old XJ6's could be bought very cheaply and our hero Gary had aspirations of modifying the car with such hideous gems as a boot spoiler and BBS alloys. However, these imaginative strokes of genius were cut short permanently when he was found dead in his garage, the apparent victim of an electric shock. The inquest heard he had been using a stolen angle grinder which had not been earthed correctly and a concerned neighbour discovered him slumped as if in the attitude of prayer by the front of his "granddad car" as it was described by said neighbour. The only witness to Gary's last moments on this earth was the brooding unkept XJ6 which was still trying to maintain an air of grandeur despite its seedy surroundings.

· · · · · · · ·

We pass into 2000 and something, and our stately old Jag is now listed on a popular online auction site "for spares". The idea here is that the seller displays a picture of the whole car on their listing and then people request various parts which are then plucked from the carcass of the vehicle. It's a grizzly end to a classic but one could argue it helps others of its kind to stay on the road.

That would be so except in this case it wasn't the end. Before our anonymous entrepreneur could dissect as much as one rusted bolt or pull one perished hose from the helpless old girls' innards - it vanished one night!

The police were called but gave the matter little of their time due to the value of the vehicle and the unsecured nature of the premises. I should mention by this time the XJ6 was known as a "non-runner". Whether this was the same night Terry Daniels spotted the graceful lady tearing up the road as if chased by the devil I cannot say, although I think not. I think the great escape from being turned into a parts bin happened earlier.

. . . .

I will end the life and times of our series 3 XJ6 Jaguar with the last known account and most recent appearance of the graceful dowager.

This harrowing ordeal was experienced by a woman in her early thirties and occurred in the early hours of a bitterly cold November night in 2016. The woman in question, we will call her Dawn had been out with friends for the night and having dropped the last of them off headed for home at a little past 1am. Not long after this her barely two-year-old car went into what's known as "limp home mode". A fault had occurred and this feature was designed to let the vehicle get you to a garage or home. The slow progress eventually ended in the vehicle grinding to a halt opposite a quiet roundabout near to the entrance of a closed industrial estate.

Staying calm and locking the doors, Dawn phoned her breakdown recovery service, giving her location was easy as it was her regular route to and from town. She was informed someone would be with her within two hours.

Just before 2am she heard the first sound of a vehicle since her own had spluttered to a halt. A white van or maybe yellow, it was difficult to see under the street lights, drove past the gated estate entrance stopped for a second then pulled up behind her own vehicle.

After what seemed an age a man wearing a hi-visibility coat disembarked from the van approached her door and tapped on the window. I'm afraid people see and hear only what they are expecting to. Dawn was waiting for a recovery van so when a van and a man appeared wearing a uniform... she willingly opened her door.

The man quickly pulled her out of the vehicle and produced a knife, giving her instructions to get into the back of his van. When all hope seemed lost her terrified eyes caught sight of a car's dim headlights not far off.

The old XJ6 4.2 rolled forward from its vantage point. It was running with only sidelights on and seemed swathed in darkness, and the tyres made a crunching sound as they rolled over the gritted road. Two huge plumes of exhaust smoke rose from the twin pipes and hung in the frozen air; the engine was just a murmur.

The startled attacker seeing the huge saloon pushed his victim to the ground and made for the driver's door of his van. In what seemed a blink of an eye the Jaguar came to life and spat vengeance at the would-be attacker. The sleek giant sped forward and blocked the man from gaining entry. The huge bonnet pointed directly at him. The engine revving hard caused the whole body to rock. He was pinned up against the van, the big Jag's chrome grill Jag touching his knee caps.

Dawn had used the distraction wisely. She returned to her car, locked the door and phoned the police on her mobile. She now watched in perplexed fascination as her would-be attacker was in turn menaced by this booming monster. With growing terror, the man managed to free himself and clamber onto the low-slung bonnet of the Jag in the hopes of running away. This move seemed to have been anticipated or even hoped for by the driver. The moment the man placed both feet on the bonnet the driver floored the accelerator. The front end lifted and the rear wheels found traction and he was catapulted against the windscreen. The jag continued to build up speed as the terrified attacker stayed pressed hard against the frozen windscreen, the night air was filled with the angry roar from the straight six engine.

The driver then slammed the brakes on hard. The attacker was propelled some thirty feet clear of the Jag. He barrel-rolled over and over on the freezing tarmac. The sound of each impact was sickening.

Dawn watched in disbelief and undying thanks as the big saloon benignly performed a U-turn and headed back towards her at a sedate pace. She wound down the window on the passenger's side expecting the car to pull alongside but was disappointed to see it glide past in a low rumble and continue on in the direction it had first appeared and was gone into the frozen night. The Jag's windows were all frosted over so both her and her attacker, who did survive but would now be doing his break down recovery impersonations with the aid of a wheel chair, could not see who was driving the antique machine.

Dawn could only add that the car's number plate was something, something 313X and to quote her directly "it was like the car that crooked car dealer drove in that tv series."

. . . .

"Something, something 313x? A stately old Jaguar lost in time and out of place in today's world of modern motoring. The one that got away - or just a case of mistaken identity? It's funny how with classic cars you only get out what you put in.

SOLITUDE

"Lincolnshire is a county with flat fertile acres, uninterrupted views and the striking Wolds. A land steeped in ancient legends and traditions. Strange echoes and phenomena from the past haunt the vast landscape and perhaps always will".

When my divorce was all said and done and both parties had fired off their salvos through their respected solicitors and a volley of letters had gone back and forth with various amendments to be made and matters finalised, I found myself alone and in search of a new place to call home. Well I say alone but not quite. Apart from my scant belongings and a bank account, I had my lumbering clod hopping four-year-old golden Labrador called Wilson. As stubborn as he was intelligent and clumsy as he was inquisitive, he was never one of the "amendments" to be finalised, he came with me regardless.

I finally opted for a small remote two bed cottage in Lincolnshire about seven miles to the north west of the historic market town of Alford. It had been a close-run contest with Norfolk. I loved both counties equally and had visited them on many occasions for holidays when I had lived in the city, but providence along with my available funds pointed me to the small cottage in Lincs first.

My cottage was so many hundred years old - I forget how many now, built of red brick but with some large areas having had rendering applied while other walls retained the locally sourced brick. There was one entrance through a tiny porch which led into the sitting room with huge dark beams and an inglenook fireplace and to the side of this a latched door leading to the stair case. The kitchen led off the lounge and was immediately on your left from the porch, it was a good size and also retained the chunky beams, many of which were festooned with large meat hooks.

The rear of the property had been extended to accommodate a bathroom. Access to this was gained by walking over what would have been the original back door step now worn into a curve in the middle, a testament to the age of the place. The narrow winding carpet-less stairs led to two small bedrooms. Access to the rear room was through the first, there was no corridor or landing. Both rooms had one window each but were not gloomy or claustrophobic. Light from the huge sky cascaded in effortlessly.

I wanted a place to hide from the world and this really did fit the bill, access to my dwelling was to be gained by turning off the lane and over a dirt cart track across a large field. This operation depended entirely on the current position and resting place, at any given time, of the grazing cows or "beasts" as I heard a local farmer call them.

The little cottage had a gated entrance and my battered estate car filled the gravelled parking space in its entirety. The land extended to half an acre of garden mostly laid to lawn with a wood shed twenty yards from the porch. The grass gently sloped downwards to a wooden bridge that spanned a stream. I was lucky enough to have negotiated and separately purchased one and a half acres of woodland from the local land owner. This extra parcel of land began almost immediately at the other end of the bridge.

My new abode kept me fully occupied and two months seemed to come and go before I knew it. I did little inside the cottage other than arrange my furniture reline the chimney to accommodate my wood burner and make the kitchen more user friendly by increasing the work surface and adding two new units. Anything else could wait until the long winter months.

The summer days drew me to the garden foremost. Wilson would disappear for hours exploring his new surroundings often reappearing out of the dense woodland covered in something unmentionable and looking thoroughly proud of himself. I found several weeks work in fencing off my small part of this majestic county with heavy staked posts and pig wire to about waist height. I also re-tiled the leaking wood shed and dug a small vegetable plot at the rear and left of the garden. The setting was made complete with a tiny cobbled together greenhouse.

Some four months into my retired solitude I had my first real encounter with a "local". I had walked back across the dirt track to collect my post. Wilson as always came with me, although that day he was on a leash owing to the "beasts" in the field. My rustic post-box was nailed to a railway sleeper where the dirt track joined the road on a slight bend and as more often than not the journey proved fruitless.

But that day we were greeted with "morning" and I turned to see an old uniformed man with an outstretched arm holding a brown coloured letter. "I'm Archie the postman" followed before I could return the salutation. I had to stifle a chuckle, the red ER van and postal uniform had tipped me off to his vocation.

Archie gave me a brief history of the immediate area. I found out my cottage had once been a popular holiday let. My closest neighbours were the Thompson's in the old station house. "Look over there, can you see the overgrown platforms?" he asked. I had noticed the house from my garden on the horizon. "They always leave the lights on all night", I chipped in. Archie let out a "Ahhhh that's to keep Black Shuck from coming too close." I looked baffled. "Padfoot" he said. The penny dropped and I laughed and told him no rural setting is complete without a spectral hound. He sniggered. Before he left, he gave me advice on the best hostelries to frequent and the name of a farm. He said that if I called in and mentioned his name, I would be given a whole salmon no questions asked. I liked Archie but I did form the impression that anything I told him would find its way round the nearest town and outlying properties before the sun was low in the sky.

Some weeks after this considerable social event in my life I was relaxing in front of the fire in my armchair. The other two-seater sofa closest to the fire, Wilson had commandeered as his own and the uncouth oaf was happily snoring, laid on his back with legs reached out. The time was a little after 11pm.

I was just thinking about letting the slumbering behemoth out to "see the rabbits" as I called it before making my way up to bed, when I heard a noise outside.

Something had scuttled past the porch and carried on down the concrete paving stones before reaching the lawn. Wilson had also heard the sound and sat up on his sofa looking towards the window. I got up and looked out. Nothing but inky blackness. I had no outside light so it was impossible to see further than the first two stones in any direction.

I grabbed my heavy four cell metal torch and with a "come on" we both ventured out into the night. Trust me, the saying "pitch black" really did this night an injustice. There was no light from the night sky not even a slight glow, no stars or moon. I managed to fix my relative position by lining up the pin prick of light from the old station house in a line with my wood shed. I shone the powerful torch round the garden as Wilson sniffed the dense air and ventured forward a few paces. I angled the beam to its most compact and it just about reached the wooden bridge, but I could see nothing. Just then Wilson left me and with his snout glued to the ground retraced his steps and hurried indoors.

"Nice," I muttered, but then came the silence. I can vouch for another old saying that silence can be deafening. As you would expect my rural hideout was always deathly quiet at night but this new silence ushered in with it an ominous brooding quality. I did not like it. I decided to follow my chums' example and head indoors. I bolted the door behind me and decided to install two solar ground lights either side of the bridge.

Wilson, who was to be found peering out from

behind his chair, big brown eyes looking sad and ears down adopted a habit that night that would stay in place the rest of his life. He abandoned his kitchen bed and instead barged past me on the stairs, quickly settling in the corner of my room by the tallboy and immediately pretending to be asleep.

Not long after this experience I had allotted a whole day to gathering fire wood. I surmised as I tramped round my forestry and over thickets that the last people to visit this place may have been holidaymakers renting my cottage. Having been a more frequent visitor to these woods than me, Wilson led the way and busied himself in finding new sniffs and careering through the ferns. The outskirts of the woods started with Willow closest to the stream, then a dense pocket of ash which gave way to ancient beech and sporadic huge oaks.

By dusk I had gathered enough fallen wood to last many months. I had pulled this collection of limbs and stumps clear of the forest and dumped them lawn side of the wooden bridge. I had made a good start with the chopping and splitting, when my aching back combined with my hungry compadre nuzzling into me, informing me to call it a day.

I woke with a start from a deep sleep. Wilson was staring at me from his sofa eyes wide with a haunted look, and the clock on the mantle informed me it was a little before one am. My days toil had obviously got the better of me and I had nodded off not long after my Salmon tea (thank you Archie). The fire was nothing more than pale embers and there was a slight chill in the room.

"Come on" I said to my nervous looking friend. We ventured out together, although looking back now I rather wish I had gone straight to bed. There was a good-sized moon out that night but drifting clouds in the vast sky kept it hidden at regular intervals and left me in profound darkness for the best part. Luckily, the white glow from the closest of my new solar lights gave me a reference and perspective in the darkness.

After no more than a minute Wilson, as before retraced his steps and hurried back inside. I was alone and once again that terrible malignant silence descended across my land and it was timed perfectly with another spell of total darkness. Before I could think of joining Wilson, I heard the sound of something crossing the wooden bridge and heading in my direction. The noise was a heavy padding and almost certainly made by four legs in contact with the damp wooden slats. It sounded similar to when my absent chum followed close behind me on walks.

The sound then ceased and I assumed the visitor had reached the lawn. The eerie silence was becoming unbearable. In my rush I had forgotten my torch and to my bemusement the white glow from the solar lights had vanished. With a horrid start I realised that I had misjudged what my eyes were telling me. The ground light hadn't gone or been put out but it was being obstructed from my sight by something.

Suddenly a pair of enormous dull orange globes materialized in the shadowy darkness. All at once I realised that in this oppressive withering silence, I was being observed by something outside my understanding. The ground light then became visible but then in a second was gone again. This thing whatever it was, must be pacing back and forth. Every so often the orange saucers glanced in my direction as the pacing continued, all to the backdrop of the detested silenced that bore into me all the time.

Finally, my curiosity as to the identification of the night caller left, and was swiftly replaced with growing terror. I fled back to my lounge and double locked the door. Wilson ran to greet me in a sheepish manor and offered licks as if to atone for leaving his post. I was quite shaken after my encounter and looked down at my stocky sidekick. "Thanks a lot friend," I said rather sharply. He tilted his head to one side while his big brown eyes looked full of sorrow. He then took himself upstairs to bed with a resounding thud. Maybe I was asking too much of him.

As three or four more years passed, this latest incident slipped further and further from my mind. I lived happily with Wilson who as time wore on pushed his luck further and indulged in more liberties. One morning I forget exactly when, I awoke to find his furry bulk hogging most of the bed. When questioned his response was a furrowed brow and a wave of his large paw. With some adjustments to our night-time rota we avoided any more encounters with the orange eyed prowler, though now and then we both sometimes thought it close by.

One Friday night in October I had been to my local

"The Railway Tavern" to compete in a dominoes match. Thanks to an ordnance survey map I had bought a few years ago, I discovered that I could get to the tavern by cutting through my woods, bearing left along a farm track for about fifteen minutes and then following the hedge line over several large fields. This would eventually bring me out at the south end of what passed for the main road just two hundred yards from the tavern. By now Wilson was feeling his age and the three odd miles to the Tavern was asking a bit much of the old boy. He was happy to stay at home and luxuriate on his sofa as usual, and I always promised to bring him back a bag of crisps.

The match dragged on at what seemed a snail's pace and I was much later leaving than normal (I usually went once or twice a month). The temperature had dropped significantly while in the tavern and a cutting wind was at my back as I made swift progress over the fields torch in hand and collar turned up. I reached the farm track just before midnight and in ten minutes a very faint outline against the bruised night sky denoted the start of my woods. As I rounded a bend which led to a steel gate, I stopped immediately.

Less than thirty feet from where I stood, those dull orange eyes were waiting on me - it had returned! My old enemy was here and now very clear to me. Whether a humungous hound or deranged dog I could not say. Black in colour with matted, scraggy fur, patchy in some places while thick and clumped around the neck. It stood legs splayed head down displaying endless glistening teeth. The torchlight seemed to pick up a faint steam rising from its tattered coat. It was as if the creature had travelled many miles over the vast open fields and was burning with exhaustion.

As with my experiences before, so too now, the horrible all-consuming brooding silence accompanied this being and for the first time since I moved to my retreat, I cursed the remoteness and my vulnerability. The thought of making a run for it clambering over the steel gate and through woodland in near total darkness seemed intolerable. The creature would cut me down in seconds I would be face to face with it and forced into a close combat situation. I switched off my big torch and turned it round in my sweaty hand to form a truncheon and decided to make a fight of it.

I stood in the silence waiting for the creature to advance on me. A few seconds elapsed as I carefully thought how I should time my first swing. I had to land the first blow! I started to panic wondering if the thing could actually be dealt a solid strike? How long could I hold it off? Just then I felt something heavy brush past my left leg and I hastily turned my torch round switched it on and flooded the area beneath me with light.... WILSON!

My old Lab stopped in front of me as if acting as a buffer zone between me and my evil antagonist. He then did something that in all my long association with the old boy I had never witnessed. He curled his flabby lips and bared his teeth. Next came a growl which seemed impossible he could have elicited. The black spectre in turn let out a guttural growl and its hateful orange eyes grew brighter and narrower. Wilson increased his warning and his stout frame advanced again, the two were now in a stand-off incomprehensible to a human being.

At last the aggressor relented and made off over the fields by way of jumping the steel gate. Every few seconds the detested orange eyes would be visible as it looked back on us. The air was filled briefly with a savage growling and then silence. Wilson raised his large head and put his nose to the wind as if to check the coast was clear.

After a few seconds he trotted towards home, squeezing through a gap in the fence. I followed shakily, throwing cautious looks behind me which did not cease until I reached my door. Once home I secured the door, which I found half ajar, and calmed my nerves with a large brandy. My chum clambered up onto his sofa and sat upright with a satisfied look on his usual lugubrious face. I walked over to him with the promised crisps, opened the bag but before relinquishing them to his giant paw, I bent down so we were eye to eye and said "Thank you Wilson." He replied with a lick on my hand then busied himself tucking into his late-night snack.

Time moved on and as nature sadly dictates, a dog's time among us is agonisingly short. Two years after this final encounter Wilson was to leave me. I hung his soft leather collar above the mantel in remembrance, I look at it often. His passing left a gap that I couldn't replace nor would want to.

I miss my friend. I miss him bounding through the garden, I miss the reassuring snoring at night when I wake from a nightmare. But I miss him most when sat alone in my arm chair in front of a glowing fire and I hear a strange sound from the fathomless darkness outside. On such occasions I look across to his sofa and a smile plays on my lips as I look at the grubby armrest closest to the fire that he would loll his head on and the rear cushion still crushed flat by his bulk over the years.

On such nights I also remember how my good friend somehow sensed I was in danger and putting aside his own fears, left the warmth and sanctuary of his beloved chair to venture out into the darkness one cold October night to stand by me.

"A man went looking for a retreat from the world and sought solitude and escape in the lonely fields of Lincolnshire…. he found these in abundance and while doing so learnt the true meaning of that old saying - a man's best friend…."

A SIGN OF DANGER

"The oceans of the world, an undulating
graveyard that cover almost three quarters of our
planet. For hundreds of years tales of idly drifting
derelict ships have been told and retold. Some of these
ghost ships were reclaimed and sailed again while
others took their invisible crews and locked up secrets
to the fathomless depths forever"

I'm filthy rich you know…. oh, and what's more… I wouldn't know a day's work if I tripped over it! I spend my time loafing about on my private yacht guzzling beer, improving my tan and sometimes strutting the deck with my white flannels, blazer and yachting cap. This look is often referred to by my few friends as "the captain Birdseye outfit."

Six years ago, trust me when I tell you I did know a day's work, a very long day which always seem to yield little in the way of remuneration. I won't bore you with my life story, it's an unremarkable tale and would find better use as a sleeping draught. I will however take you back to those six years ago and explain just how I became wealthy and, in the process, more understanding of that which defies explanation.

Back then I was owner/operator of my own tug boat the "Cyclops" and she was available for emergency ocean towage work or coastal charter. The Cyclops displaced 58 tons with an overall length of 35 meters, beam of ten meters and draft of five meters. She was steel hulled, powered by two Ruston diesel engines putting out around 3760 HP, and the bow thruster was 560 HP. I won't go into endless technical jargon about the brake capacities, tugger winches, deck cranes etc.

My business made a tepid start but eventually I did secure some big contracts and I thought my luck had changed. However, I was released from these contracts after several mechanical failures resulted in the tug spending long spells in dry dock. I usually crewed with six men and most of whom had worked with me before. During another lengthy overhaul and replacement of some auxiliary equipment, I was forced to lay all my crew off for the "foreseeable future" they were ok about it and were adept at finding other work on similar tugs.

With no change in my fortunes and having missed the last four payments on the Cyclops, I finally decided to throw in the towel after a routine job towing a barge ended in its sinking.

During rough seas the tow line broke and the 300-foot steel welded barge drifted helplessly. The waves pounded the fiberglass covers and in no time, it had disappeared from sight in the swirling turbulent foam.

A week after the sinking I was sat in a pub drowning my sorrows and really not in the mood for company. By chance a man called Faulkner came in. I had employed him a couple of times aboard Cyclops but really knew very little about him. He got a drink from the bar and came over to the dingy corner where I was rapidly becoming "three sheets to the wind".

After a few pleasantries and offering his condolences pertaining to my current situation (word about the barge sinking had got around fast). He then randomly blurted out "They just found the Lady Patricia." I snorted in my beer and replied "What again?" Faulkner looked indignant at this and started telling me all about how the sighting wasn't far from here.

I should point out that the Lady Patricia was a bulk carrier of "Handysize". This is a naval term used for smaller bulk carriers with a deadweight of between 10,000 and 50,000 tonnes typically. Lady Patricia was 150 meters in length with five cargo holds (number one being closest to the bow) and four 30 metric ton cranes for cargo handling. She was due for scrapping and had broken free to avoid her date with the cutters torch some four months earlier! Since then she had been seen on a few occasions drifting aimlessly and even taken in tow once. After the last failed attempt, she had been thought sunk, apparently until now....

"Got enough time to hear me out?" Faulkner said from the bar.

"Go on"

As if to sweeten the offer, he returned with a pint in each hand and gave one to me.

"Get that down you."

I thanked him and he hastily told me the following account.

Faulkner had been a junior officer onboard the Lady Patricia and completed several cruises. After the second cruise he realised something wasn't right on the ship. Some of the crew would play big money poker games with little care for the outcome, and if they lost, it was marked against the "next voyages take." On one occasion he saw a mere deck hand leave the dock for home in a Bentley! While a pot washer in the galley seemed to be sporting a damn fine Rolex, which he plunged into the dirty suds and greasy pans with an air of complete abandonment.

It soon became clear that there was some sort of elite within the crew and the common theme within this group was a surfeit of wealth! Faulkner did his best to watch the comings and goings of certain individuals, but not all were so brazen about their lavish second income. He narrowed the field of suspects down to 8 or 9 from a crew of 31. After Faulkner had put in a full year onboard, tongues began to loosen and it was a junior engineer who filled in the blanks for him. There was, as he correctly surmised an extremely lucrative smuggling racket in progress. Faulkner had assumed drugs, but he was wrong. The engineer's childlike description of the contraband was "shiny goodies and sparklers".

On most voyages the ship would have three large steel boxes hidden onboard in different locations. Depending how high the persons involvement in the scam was, denoted their knowing the location of all three hiding places. Faulkner's informer knew of only one of the hiding places: the engine room. Apparently, it was so well concealed that those in the know had lost all fear of it ever being found. Faulkner pressed him further but he was starting to get suspicious and got little more information other than the secret compartment was in a bulkhead near something always in use and moving so as to avoid unnecessary contact.

A few days after the ship docked and he had learned enough from eavesdropping on various conversations to know that the boxes were onboard. They must have been damned good at getting it stowed and past the Captain, who he was fairly sure was ignorant of the whole thing. He decided to hang about the ship on the pretext of some delay with his leave arrangements. The valuables would at some point have to be surreptitiously unloaded.

Before he got a chance to try his hand at detective the ship had been seized, all crew ordered off and everything sealed. Of course, the most obvious conclusion sprang to his mind.... the game was up! But no, a much more mundane answer was to blame for the impounded ship and one I can totally sympathise with.

The company who owned the Lady Patricia and three other similar vessels had gone into receivership not long after they had put to sea. They had not been informed whilst at sea as the receivers thought an angry crew, knowing that they were unlikely to be paid when they made port, might just abandon the vessel or even become tempted to steal various items from the ship.

Lady Patricia was towed to a secure mooring out of the way while the receivers found a buyer for the vessel. The crew were allowed back on to collect their belongings but were escorted at all times. When the carrier went for survey she was found to be in poor condition, which as you can imagine did little to induce a buyer and after languishing for 18 months she was sent for scrapping.

I interrupted him at this point and obnoxiously said I knew all the rest, she broke away while on transit to the breakers, she drifted she was found blah blah blah. I then thanked him for his take on Treasure Island and ushered him towards the door.

He assumed a red hue, got up and raised his voice "Has it not got through to you?"

I said nothing but went on drinking. He continued as if arguing his point in a court case. Summarising his findings, he closed his speech by pointing out that the Lady Patricia was last seen not too far away, she was classed as a derelict. I had a tug that could reach her and there was a fortune onboard that would never be missed! We ordered coffee and sandwiches and I cross examined him at length.

"How do you know that the contraband is still onboard?

"The ship has been impounded and was sealed the moment it docked. And the crew only went back onboard once and they were escorted the whole time," he replied.

I then asked about the recent sighting of the ship.

"They picked up a signal from her emergency position-indicating radio beacon, and as you know they only start transmitting when they are exposed to water," he explained.

"Yeh, but that could mean that she has already sunk," I chipped in.

"No, a helicopter was sent up in response and they saw her. She was still in international waters then," he confirmed.

Despite his hard sell I was struggling with the whole idea and I had become morose again. It was at that point Faulkner said something that woke me from my lethargy. "We all know this time next week you won't even have the Cyclops anymore. I bet a few days after that you will be swinging a mop about on a freighter feeling sorry for yourself." That stinging comment hit me hard and Faulkner got his desired result…. I was in!

The cyclops was underway four hours after Faulkner's sales spiel in the pub, and everything we were likely to need was already onboard. We had selected two other men to undertake the "salvage" operation. Winters and Brown, I had worked with them more times than most others I knew and I felt sure they would fall in with the idea. Once at sea both the other men were brought into our confidence.

It didn't take long to reach the location where the transmitter signal had been picked up. I told the others that the device was probably in a lifeboat that had been torn from its cradle in a bad storm – that wasn't unheard of. From this point we followed the most logical course a drifting ship would take allowing for the weather and currents. On the bridge I briefed the other three for about the tenth time since we left harbour.

Brown would remain on the Cyclops throughout the operation, bringing us in close so we could climb aboard and then keep clear. I presumed the ship would be empty and sitting high in the water and had the necessary equipment ready if we needed to scale the hull. The rest of us would then hoist the equipment up and all head directly for the only known location of one of the concealed boxes: the engine room. Brown was to be our eyes and ears and keep in touch by walkie-talkie the whole time. It wouldn't take long before other vessels would be despatched to take the carrier in tow. By now the drifting hulk had been declared a hazard to shipping.

The battered profile of the Lady Patricia came into view off the starboard bow. I scanned the area with binoculars to check for other vessels before doing anything else. Good I thought nothing in sight. That was the first hurdle cleared. Then followed a disappointment, the binoculars revealed the carrier was listing to port about ten degrees and down at the bow. She looked like she might be taking on water fast. The thought of being in a pitch-black maze of companionways and passages below decks on a 492-foot carrier shipping water was a sobering thought. I asked Faulkner if the Lady Patricia was double hulled, he said she was. That would buy us time. I ordered Brown to slowly circle the vessel once, then all being well, gently take the cyclops in on the port side near the super structure as the rest of us sorted the equipment.

Soon we were alongside the weathered blue hull of the drifting derelict looking up at the four huge faded yellow cranes streaked with rust. A broken tow line was trailing, and we also noted signs of a recent collision. Both anchors were missing. Nothing seemed to stir other than inquisitive seagulls overhead and several loose cables swaying rhythmically from two of the inert cranes. Then at times came an ominous creaking from below decks.

Winters then called out "I've seen someone on the flying bridge we're too damn late" (This was the open area on top of the ship that gives an unobstructed view). My heart sank as I hurriedly glanced up and scanned the area...I could see no one, then Brown and Faulkner confirmed they could also see nothing. I curtly reminded Winters no other ships were in the area and no boats were tied up alongside the carrier. Winters was adamant he had seen someone for a brief second but could make out nothing more than a silhouette. I shrugged this off as nerves and ordered him and Faulkner to get ready to board.

Owing to the carriers list to port we were able to board her without any problems. The bridge of the cyclops came to more or less level with the deserted deck and by timing it right, soon all three of us and the equipment were left watching the cyclops pull away. I reminded the other two to watch out for rats...I had seen huge hoards of them on derelicts before. By the way, I had told Brown before I disembarked to sound the fog horn and keep sounding it if it looked like the ship was in danger of going down.

Before making for the engine room I changed my mind and wanted to look for the ships plans - they could save a lot of time once down in the darkness below decks.

Plans are a must if a crew are to deal with problems that they are likely to encounter during the lifetime of a vessel, and particularly as she becomes older. They will require three sets of a ship's plans, or drawings, with the master retaining a 'best' set, and chief mate and chief engineer each keeping a working set. From my experience framed copies of some of the most important plans are likely to be displayed upon bulkheads within the accommodation.

Faulkner led the way to the Captain's cabin and we made an extensive search but no plans for the engine room were forthcoming. We noted, however, that the whole cabin had already been heavily ransacked. Next, we silently made our way to the Captain's day room and continued the search. A levered open filing cabinet in the corner yielded results. The top drawer was empty but the bottom two were crammed with a plethora of diagrams, charts, drawings you name it: Capacity plan, trimming tables, Cargo Ventilation plan, the GA plan, Bulkhead plans, and finally stuffed between safety procedures and a Midship Section plan there was a detailed layout of the engine room also containing a large diagram.

With time pressing we forwent going to the bridge and made our way down to the lower decks. About this time, I noticed a change in Faulkner. We were all anxious and I admit quite frankly uneasy but he bore a look of nervousness bordering on downright terror. I radioed Brown on the Cyclops and told him we were heading to the engine room, he acknowledged and said all was quiet.

We hadn't gone far when I stopped and craned my head upwards. The other two looked at me impatiently.

"Shh!" I said, I could hear shuffling footsteps above us. We stood silently in the dank passageway listening… There was a scurrying from further down and I could hear dripping water close by.

"Someone is up there" Winters said in a croaky voice. The three of us stood motionless waiting… Any second I expected someone to come down the stairs we had just descended from. Nothing but the creaking of hull plates as the abandoned ship continued its drift.

I quelled Winters fears and said it was just the way the ship was moving and being out of trim. It did sound like footsteps I will admit but I also have to ashamedly confess I was burning up with gold fever by this stage, and to get me off the old bulk carrier empty handed would have taken a loaded gun at my head. Faulkner's unease was growing…

The engine room was as black as pitch and shin deep in heavy fuel oil and sea water. Under the influence of our powerful torch beams it took on a grotesque setting. A tangled maze of rusted pipes, corroded machinery and scattered tools. The centre piece amid this frightening chaos was the enormous main engine or prime mover. A huge six-cylinder two stroke diesel engine. Aft of the main engine there were three auxiliary diesel generators and close by the A.C plant and condenser. There were also three storage compartments and a workshop. Overlooking all of this on a steel gantry next to a walkway and ladders where we now stood, was a large auxiliary boiler. The once busy heart of the ship with endless activity, changes of watch and deafening cacophony of engines and machinery was now a nerve jangling silent putrid steel sarcophagus.

"We must be mad" said Winters surveying the

carnage from the gantry looking down into the depths with one hand clamped to the railing in a vice like fashion while the other was busy with the torch. I ignored his comment and started to descend the narrow steps into the filthy water. There we stood alongside the main engine in total darkness, and in very nearly knee-deep oily brine, looking for god knows what, on a ship that could sink any minute. If that wasn't enough Winters then announced that the walkie-talkie was dead and we should leave!

"Stop flapping!" I barked at him. "I thought those cheap radios might not work once we got all the way down here, why do you think I asked Brown to sound the horn if the ship looked in real trouble?" Before he could elicit a reply, I followed this up with "Brown's got our back, you can hear that damn horn miles away so let's get on!"

I told them to search the area by the diesel generators and to take crow bars and hammers. If they suspected anything, I told them not to be shy about giving it the 'knock test' we hadn't time to play this cool. Before they left, I reminded them that the hiding place was ingenious but still had to be accessible and allow a good-sized box to be hidden. That was according to Faulkner's informer anyway. If they suspected a void or false bulkhead - consult the plans before wasting too much time.

They waded off into the darkness while I headed over to the air conditioning unit. I was hell bent on recovering the box but the enormity of the task was starting to sink in. I shined the torch on my watch. So far, we had been onboard for 27 minutes. If only we had more to go on!

For the next 35 minutes we examined every bulkhead that the diagrams suggested might have enough room to stow something in or behind. We went over every panel, crawl space, duct and conduit possible. We tore down pipework, fire extinguishers and racks. Anything we remotely suspected of being a suspect was tapped and bashed. Nothing! No tell-tale new welds, no false doors, no disturbed rust and no luck!

"Take a break," I told the other two. I made my way over to them and straight away asked Faulkner if he was sure about the box being near some sort of moving parts. He nodded while looking nervous and shining his torch round the blackness trying to pin point the creaks and groans as the ship pitched a little.

I left Winters and Faulkner to continue the search telling them I would be back in 10 minutes; I needed to radio Brown on the Cyclops and update him. I retraced my steps to B deck and tried the walkie-talkie, Brown answered immediately and sounded stressed. I updated him as to the situation so far. He said the carrier was down at the bow more and the fore peak tank, deck store and thruster room were all now under the surface. I acknowledged and told him I would radio in again in 30 minutes. As long as cargo hold one keeps watertight, we have enough time I thought.

Brown cut in again and asked why we keep fiddling about on the bridge??

"No one's been up there" I replied. A long silence followed; I could feel the hairs on the back of my neck stand up as I knew what was coming. He reported seeing one if not two figures moving about through the windows. Then he finished by saying "I think you have company on that crate, call it a day"

I had started down the stairs again on my way back to the engine room when I got the distinct impression I was being watched. In conjunction with this unnerving sensation I once again thought I could hear footsteps. I plucked up my courage and called out.... Somewhere far off a door slammed. I hadn't time to waste chasing mysteries but I still found myself bounding up the stairs and throwing open doors. Recreation room, the mess and a few cabins all in good order and indicated nothing that could give credence to the sightings and footsteps.

Another door slamming shut this time closer then another, then silence. The ship pitched and rolled a little and I began to feel nervous. I scanned my surroundings once more with the torch and then hurried to the engine room.

I found Winters and Faulkner looking over the main engine and they quizzed me frantically. I decided not to give them chapter and verse but only that Brown had reported the ship was down a bit more.

"Let's call it off" Faulkner pale and his eyes watery.

"Now who's giving in?" I retorted. I told them both we would stay another 30 minutes and to continue the search. I then informed them both that anyone leaving now would be giving up their share.

I asked about the workshop, and they reported they hadn't searched it yet. I told them not to bother with the main engine. The workshop was practically dry due to it being on the starboard side of the ship. It was good to get away from breathing fuel fumes for a bit. There were two large lathes at the far end, drill presses and grinders along the longest bulkhead. Several other machines had broken free and were laying in a contorted heap on the steel floor while a large bandsaw had toppled over and was precariously leaning on the main work bench in the centre of the compartment.

We fanned out and commenced yet another search pattern, bulkheads were examined metal lockers scrutinized and tool chests tipped over. Still nothing!

Winters stopped his efforts and shone his torch over at me. "We thought we saw someone up above while you were gone" he said in a whisper. I told him to keep looking and to try by the lathes. He asked me if I had heard what he said. I suspended my fruitless examinations briefly and shone my torch directly at Faulkner. "I think you left out some details about this old bucket in your presentation!" Before he could reply the ship let out a cracking sound and we all felt the angle of list increase.

After another five minutes I hurled a massive spanner into the darkness and started cursing. The tool ricocheted off the far bulkhead and the crash echoed through the darkness. I slumped onto one of the lathes exhausted. It had all been for nothing! A complete farce! Skulking around an unwholesome ship that could at any moment drag us to the sea floor. I bashed my hands down on the metal lathe bed and recoiled at once in pain. The bed was covered in razor sharp metal swarf and turnings, some floating in a nearly dried up puddle of cutting fluid.

"Did you search round here?" I shouted at Winters. He said it all looked ok. "Bring your torches over here" I told them.

Under the added light I examined the lathe and the neighbouring one. The one directly in front of me was a very old model (I had something similar on the Cyclops when I first took her on). The other lathe nearby must have been new or nearly new at the time of the ship's last voyage. I wondered why the new one had not been used on her last voyage and why the far more inferior older model had evidently been hard at work judging by the swarf. I pointed this out to the other two who offered reasons like perhaps the new one had broken down or someone just liked using the older one.

I shone my torch on the bulkhead behind the lathes. There were several tools fixed to them followed by a series of large warning signs displayed prominently at just above head height.

The sign directly behind the older lathe bore the legend "EAR PROTECTION MUST BE USED" and a caricature of a head with ear defenders in place. There was a dent just above the word 'ear' where the spanner had left its mark. The gash revealed the paint looked new under a film of grime. I examined the sign close up and then once again double checked what I had seen behind the machine.

"Bring the tools over and pull this sign down" I told Winters. They both looked aghast and demanded we all leave. I replied "NOW"

Winters started to lever the sign off the bulkhead, and I asked Faulkner a question as he held the torch on the subject.

"Did you ever have a model railway as a kid?"

"No I didn't," he replied bitterly and understandably looked at me as if I had gone raving mad.

"I was a keen modeller until I was about 13, and do you know what one of the hardest parts of making models is?" I calmly asked him.

He did not reply, just the groaning of the ship and the sound of Winters at work. Before he could lash out at me or suggest I should see someone, I answered my own question.

"Weathering" I said.

"What?" he replied impatiently.

"Well if you want to make a locomotive look old or as if it has been hard at work for months a keen modeller would "weather" it. Too much and it looked false and tacky, - too little would look unconvincing. Now that sign you're pulling down and is about to join the rest of the debris on the deck, has most certainly been weathered to look years old," I explained to him.

"But it might be though" he fumed.

The sign in question bore a new design and, in the bottom left corner was the manufacturers name, copyright and a date which tied in with the date Faulkner gave for the very last voyage. That combined with a very old lathe that seemed to still be hard at work while a much better model was feet away had aroused my suspicions. The sign came free in two pieces and fell onto the invisible blackness of the floor. Then all torches were aimed at where it had once been....

The white beams were met with a perfectly square outline of neat weld. Roughly 30 inches squared. I ordered Faulkner to bring the battery powered angle grinder over and start work. The weld beads looked new even allowing for the condition of the ship.

Just then came the muffled but clear sound of the horn from the Cyclops! Winters turned to leave. It was now or never - it had simply gone too far to turn back. I screamed at Faulkner to start cutting the welds.

"She's going down now!" he protested.

I reassured him firmly that we had time to complete the job and it could just be to warn us another vessel had turned up. (I could tell from the increasing angle the ship didn't have long). I consulted the drawings as the shrill sound of the angle grinder started up. It was a transverse bulkhead that divided this section of the ship from Number 5 cargo hold on the other side.

Minutes seemed like hours as the grinder worked its way round the side of the welded outline all the while the creaking and complaining from the old carrier grew louder. Every few seconds came another blast from the Cyclops. If the angle carried on increasing the old carrier would break her back. After a change of battery and a new disc the welds had finally all been cut. Winters in a panic clumsily pried the newly created panel free and with a resounding clatter it hit the deck.

I craned into the portal and flooded it with light. It went back no more than four feet with a slight drop towards the back. I felt a sickness and disbelief hit me; the void was empty!

No wait… There was the top of something at the back in the recess, it was just proud of the false floor. As if in a poker game playing out my final hand, I squeezed my head and shoulders into the darkness for a better look.

To my absolute undying relief and unimaginable joy, I found a grubby steel box or canister that had been pushed right to the back of the compartment. It had telling scrape marks and was now sitting in the deeper section with the lid very nearly flush with the welded floor.

With my last strength I managed to lever the square box up with the big crow bar just enough for a handle to come into view. I frantically threaded a chain through the handle exited the void and gave the command to all pull. There was some weight to the box which at least meant it contained something. After three pulls the box was clear and smashed down onto the lathe. Faulkner and Winters took a handle each, while I led the way with the torch and helped them up the stairs.

The ship was flooding fast and the angle was making progress slow. Stairs were tripped up and stumbled over and seemed to take forever to traverse. Several times we lost our footing and were flung against railings. Once out of the engine room abyss I took Faulkner's place and he negotiated us along the splintering gangway which felt like it would burst open any minute. Finally, we reached the main accommodation stairs.

"Someone is on the stairs" Faulkner called to us. I asked if it was Brown, maybe he had come to find us. Faulkner said not. I put my end of the box down and looked at the direction of the shaking beam of light. I briefly caught sight of a white face staring down at us then it disappeared as if stepping back into the stairwell. "Keep going up the stairs!" I screamed hoping whatever it was wasn't about to ambush us.

The air grew heavy and the torches started to faulter and then died, from here on we were in darkness. Footsteps seemed to be all around us as we continued our fumbling journey. I could feel rats scurrying past my ankles also looking for an escape. At times a whispering filled my ear and unidentified objects brushed past me with a swift silent motion. Just as we had been pushed beyond our limits, we reached B deck and out into the blinding light of day.

Brown had already positioned the Cyclops alongside as close as possible for which I will always be eternally grateful. I looked towards the bow of the carrier; the turquoise sea was lapping well past Number 2 hold already.

The first crane had already half disappeared.

Winters climbed aboard the tug first and tossed a rope over, which I secured around the box - just in case it slipped. Faulkner crossed next - then came an anxious fumble with the box before it landed with a thud safely on Cyclops. With one last glance up at the towering superstructure of the doomed vessel I left it and its phantasmal occupants to their fate.

Not wanting to be spotted by any other ships who might be coming to the area, Brown got us away from the hulk as soon as possible. The rest of us lay heaped in chairs on the bridge covered in oil, too exhausted and too tired to even attempt to open the battered box. Instead we glanced at one another and returned stares of total incredulity....

The thing about owning gold and diamonds is you are not rich until you sell them, you are merely in possession of valuable items which need careful handling. We were to learn this over the coming months. I say this because when I gave Faulkner the honour of opening our hard-fought trophy on the journey home that is exactly what we found!

Roughly hewn gold nuggets, pressed platinum, silver, large amounts of foreign currency and the motherload, 50 neatly folded paper squares each containing 10 flawless diamonds of 2.72 carat.

A day later we stowed our treasure securely at a place I knew while we planned our next move. The thought of leaving it on the Cyclops made me roar with laughter. I could just compose myself long enough to tell the others that the receivers were coming for the tug in a few days. If we had hidden the box onboard this whole situation would start all over again with the Cyclops being the new Lady Patricia!

I should point out that Faulkner hadn't escaped my questioning and during the hours before reaching port after we had examined our booty and recovered, I asked him to tell me the real story behind the Lady Patricia not the salesman's version....

Faulkner with the aid of quarter of a bottle of brandy took heart of courage and with Brown and Winters now avid listeners related the following account. He ashamedly admitted he had never been a member of the crew on the Lady Patricia! A stunned silence followed... Winters then piped up, pointing out how he seemed to know his way around the old bulk carrier well enough though...

"Go on with your revelations" I dryly told Faulkner, and he did so. He had got the information from a distant cousin who was in fact a genuine junior officer on the ship and had innocently stumbled upon the smuggling racket as already described. Faulkner took another swig of brandy as if to steady his nerves then looked round at all three of us and landed another shock at our already open mouths. "I've boarded the Lady Patricia before as part of a tow crew". Winters spoke for all of us with the perfectly timed comment: "For God's sake!"

It transpired that Faulkner already knowing of the stash through his cousin had volunteered to be part of the salvage crew who had tried towing the ship back for scrapping several months earlier. The ship was in better order then and could have easily been recovered. He and five others had been left as a skeleton crew onboard while she was taken in tow.

"Remember the trailing tow line? That was ours" he added sourly.

I motioned him to pass the brandy down and carry on.

His idea had been to explore the engine room at his leisure, and with only a few men onboard, the slow trip back would have given him plenty of time. He had made a search of the Captain's cabin then but then events started to happen which curtailed any other form of investigation.

The six of them knew something wasn't right with the ship from the moment they boarded her. Doors would open and close seemingly for no reason, and they all heard footsteps and voices. An atmosphere of foreboding had worn them down to the point that no one left each other's company. By the second night things had got so bad that someone (without Faulkner's knowledge) had radioed over and asked to be taken off the ship as they could stand no more. Their skipper was furious and demanded an explanation for the request.

When told about events onboard the skipper of the tug who was a devout Christian refused point blank to let anyone leave, what's more, he launched a motor dinghy and came over to the ship to give them a talking to. After a truly biblical dressing down he then decided to search the ship himself for a stowaway or two. After hearing the sounds for himself he set off alone below deck to put a stop to all the "foolhardiness" as he called it.

"About thirty minutes later the skipper re-joined us on the stern. He had looked 10 years older with the complexion of putty, shoulders sagged, hands shaking and a cigarette drooping from his lips. He ordered the First Officer aboard the emergency towing vessel to cut the tow line at once and then to come alongside to pick us up. He wouldn't hear of anyone going to the bow to release the line from the towing point and collecting the messenger line. I know that it's standard practice not to be on the bow when towing for safety reasons but that wasn't what bothered him. All he wanted was for us all to leave the bulk carrier – he was bordering on hysteria. As we waited to leave, we could hear him muttering- let her drift and sink, let her sink – his face was still ashen."

Faulkner swirled the last of his drink round in the glass and finished his incredible tale.

"I could do nothing, and before I could set about further searches or even let another member of the crew in on it, the skipper had arrived and ordered us all off and the tow line cut. To this day I wonder what he saw to make him give that order".

Finishing his brandy, he apologised out loud for his bending of the truth. In fairness to him I had to agree with his reasoning. If he had brokered the idea of a treasure hunt on a seemingly haunted ship that was sinking with only the say so of a long distant cousin to go on, I would have probably been rather "cross".

"Now let me ask you something" Faulkner boldly boomed under the influence of the brandy.

"The lathe.... wasn't that all a bit tenuous"? I drained my glass of Brandy and found another bottle and set about pouring it. I made them all wait before I offered up my reasoning...

The box had to be near moving parts, I eliminated a secret compartment in the main engine and any smaller auxiliary units. There probably wasn't room and also if they suffered any kind of failure a strip down and overhaul by someone not in on the scam would soon lead to discovery.

The lathe was a fluke I admitted. When I examined the bed as I already pointed out it had been well used and was covered in metal turnings. I also noticed a set of footprints at the rear of the bed covered partly in more turnings, and these were suggestive. These led me to the safety sign, as it was the only thing above the lathe. I take it you two didn't noticed the sign above the older lathe was riveted onto the bulk head in no less than six places? The rest were merely stuck on. I looked behind the lathe and noticed two more identical new signs hidden each with six pre drilled holes.

I finished my lecture by surmising that when removing the sign to retrieve the box even if done carefully could distort it, or like we found out break it completely. So, another identical one would always be at hand. Should anyone have ever wanted to inspect the workshop for any reason, I would bet you a platinum bar or three that someone would always be conveniently busy on the lathe making lots of mess.

To this day I keep this yellowed newspaper clipping in my wallet:

"Derelict bulk carrier Lady Patricia finally sinks after months adrift".

"The coast guard and crew of a salvage vessel have strongly denied claims that people were left onboard the hulk after she sank in deep water amid growing environmental concerns.

The argument came about after the crew of another emergency towing vessel also at the scene reported briefly seeing people onboard.

The coast guard responded saying they were the first to reach the bulk carrier but on arrival at the scene discovered she had broken in half. The bow sank immediately while the remaining stern section stayed afloat for roughly an hour.

As far as they were concerned the ship was unmanned having been abandoned months earlier after a failed recovery"

THE GHOSTS OF RAF WOODLANDS

Wartime airfields, massive infrastructures of
concrete and steel that one nation builds to destroy
another. Bubbling with emotion, drama, isolation and
sorrow. When hostilities end and the bases are vacated
to await their demise, the hustle and bustle are replaced
with an incongruous silence....

What a dismal chapfallen sight greeted me on that early Norfolk October morning in 1948. I clambered out of the transport and surveyed the disused airfield from the main gate while my kit was hastily unloaded.

Everything was grey - the sky came down to meet the soaking runways and hard standings with no apparent dividing line. The buildings matched the colour scheme with a forsaken feeling. Rain came in sheets blowing from the west with slight swirls of mist to add to the bleak unforgiving atmosphere. The hangars and Watch Office, commonly known as the Control Tower stood gaunt and silent while numerous other buildings greeted me with cracked windows festooned with cobwebs and flaking paint. Then came glimpses of past residents such as a rusting bicycle still propped up against a building, waiting for an owner who would never return. This was RAF Woodlands...

My temporary new home was the old Guard Room at the entrance to the base and seemed to convey two overriding thoughts in my mind as I explored the base a little while later.

One, was of great activity and hardships having just ceased. Almost as if a door had just closed on frantic labour and endless preparation. One could be forgiven for thinking that the service men and women who were once stationed to this remote outpost, had simply popped out for a few minutes and would soon return, rather like being in a theatre by oneself.

The second thought, and one which tied in with so many now unwanted airfields that were at the time littering the landscapes and heartlands, was that of abandonment and decay. The weeds advance on the runways and dispersals, the rust streaked Nissan huts with the stark insight they afforded into the living conditions endured by many. The crumbling ubiquitous maycrete structures. Although this was still a fully intact airfield, Mother Nature and the elements were claiming it back.

I had been stationed at another nearby RAF base and had been ordered to this disused site to man various entrances and patrol the site ready for it to be reactivated as part of flying training exercises known as 'circuits and bumps'. This was, as the name implies circuits of the airfield followed by a brief touch down and taxi and then take off again. The hazard in this type of exercise was the risk of near misses or actual accidents between the more and less experienced pilots. So, it had been decided to briefly reactivate a disused airfield for the most dangerous phase of training.

Only the main runway and a few other buildings would be needed along with the Control Tower, one hangar and the Medical Centre. I would be stationed in the old Guard Room, so I made myself as comfortable there as possible. More of my comrades were billeted at other entrances to the base but for the best part I was alone.

I knew little about the base at the time other than its name "Woodlands". As far as I was aware it had been closed to flying not long after Victory in Europe, having been deemed surplus to requirement like so many other bases. Since the events of which I am about to relate, I have dug a little bit deeper in to history of this airfield. And much of which I discovered has certainly shed some light on certain happenings.

RAF Woodlands had been a standard operational heavy bomber airfield; the runways were laid in the familiar letter A shape. The main one being 2000 yards long and in the direction of the prevailing wind with a subsidiary runway each side of about 1400 yards long. These were at an angle of 60 degrees to the main one. The runways did not have a common interaction as this would have led to all three being put out of action if an aircraft became disabled or a bomb detonate on an interaction. All were connected by a 50-foot-wide perimeter track with dispersals running off this. A notable navigation landmark was a large concrete water tower located in the closest village to the base at 050 degrees, five and a half miles.

Air Ministry policy usually meant that any new airfield took its name from the parish in which it was situated. They could also be known locally by other names. However, Woodlands took its name from the large dense forest that bordered it on two sides. To this end some of the technical and all of the domestic sites took advantage of this natural cover and nestled in its gloomy depths while the bomb storage area was located as far as possible from the main buildings on the other side of the site. In all, this made the airfield a widely dispersed site - not to mention a lonely one.

The base became an operational satellite to the already mentioned nearby base in late 1942 under the formation of 5th group Morton Hall. Personnel listed at its busiest period were as follows: R.A.F: Officers 112, S.N.C. O'S: 370, O. R'S: 1261. Total: 1743.

W.A.A.F: Officers: 10, S.N.C. O'S: 20, O.R.'S: 339. Total: 369

For over two years Woodlands took the fight to Germany this included many bombing missions in the infamous Ruhr Valley. Losses were high for the first year but not all were at German hands. Over the course of its brief career there were several tragic accidents that befell bomb-laden Lancasters struggling to get airborne with their deadly cargo or battle-weary planes limping home. Two such accidents were attributed to tyre blow outs that sent the mighty planes careering across the runways - one exploded when the undercarriage collapsed, killing all onboard, while the other hit a building with the same lethal results.

It was well known the base was badly located and adverse weather could close in rapidly. On one occasion a bomber returning home on two engines requested permission to land but was abruptly denied. The other bombers had landed but this straggler had now become a victim of the much-hated mist that barrelled in speedily from the forestry and had enveloped the site.

The aircraft was diverted but this was to prove fatal. The struggling bombers port outer engine then failed during banking and it plummeted in seconds into the dense tree canopies killing all onboard and three off-duty personnel on the domestic site. There was much anger at the order to divert the plane especially on its final approach and when damaged.

After this tragedy and other incidents, a growing sense of unease regarding this sickly fast-moving detested mist began to occupy the base commander's minds. Action was taken. The base became fitted with the FIDO system sometime in 1944 (Fog Investigation and Dispersal Operation). This consisted of two pipelines that ran the length of the runway through which copious amounts of fuel where pumped from the bases own fuel dump. The fuel was pumped into jets and then set on fire with a series of burners producing huge walls of flame.

The FIDO system had met with reasonable success on other airfields with similar issues but on Woodlands it could only ever be deemed hit and miss. The fog that seeped from the damps of the forestry and blanketed the runways, always seemed to come without warning and likewise exit the scene in a similar fashion.

The airfield in its last active days still suffered from poor and sporadic changes in weather conditions. This often meant that tired air crews returning home found themselves being diverted to other airfields. This often could, and often did lead to tragic accidents. The base also had the dubious task of storing obsolete bombers destined to be scrapped after hostilities. The ground crew worked tirelessly round the clock to make ready the massive worn out machines, some still showing signs of battle damage and repair work. They knew that the fatigued crews would nurse them home having bombed their targets in flak filled skies constantly watching for dreaded enemy night fighters.

A day or so after taking up my new duties I had let the last of the contractors off site after they had worked hard making repairs to the runway and the selected hangar to be used. I locked the barrier after them and put a check call through reporting the site was now empty.

After a cup of tea and a sandwich I decided I might have a wander around having grown bored of the austere Guard Room. I stood for a moment staring at a small wooden cupboard with bunches of keys neatly sitting on hooks. I ran my finger along them until I saw 'Control Tower'. I picked up the keys and decided to have a look around the building. This random action born of boredom was to cast a shadow over my life, which together with other events I experienced, still lingers to this day.

The Control Tower was of course going to be pressed back into service for the duration of the training, although never to full capacity as it had been used during its wartime command. At present there was no power laid to the building, it had been locked up since the base was mothballed and placed into care and maintenance. I was yet to see any sign of care or maintenance. Had everyone forgotten this place?

The tower was the most common war time design type-12779/41 with an added glasshouse perched on top. The building had two levels and if I remember correctly the bottom level usually included a meteorological office whilst upstairs was of course the flying control room. Close to the tower was the fire tender house type – 5342/42 this seem to be in a better state of repair and I planned to look this over the next day.

The tower stood stark and austere against the wispy sky - an unsightly concrete box with rust spattered railings and a short life of sorrow to impart. I had approached the building from the front elevation and was now standing directly underneath the balcony studying the outside stairs on the next level going up to the compact weather-beaten glass house. I carried on eyeing the building as I made way round to the rear entrance, keys in hand. The building returned my stare with its grey barren features and melancholy affiliations. For some reason I found myself harbouring a good deal of pity towards the concrete carbuncle with its standard austerity design and strange assortment of windows.

The wind had risen by now and the frayed pathetic-looking windsock standing a little way off flapped and strained under its influence. It was a welcome distraction because I had now reached the rear door and stood there, key in the lock staring at the peeling paint. I waited - surely that was a sound from inside? A slight indistinct thud followed by an echo? I checked the lock - yes it was locked. And now another sound came - a shuffle but farther off.

I found myself trying to fathom and calculate what I had heard, running scenarios as to what to do once inside the building. I unlocked the door and opened it. Towers of this design were typically all of the same layout, in front of me was a corridor leading towards the front of the building with rooms leading off while immediately on my right was the stairs going to the next level. As marked by a worded box with the legend 'To Flying Control' and an arrow pointing upwards.

The stillness was unbroken, no renewal of the sounds, with the wind at my back and the continuing din of the windsock still making its presence known, I stepped inside…

Immediately I was aware of a stuffy humid atmosphere that pervaded the building. This seemed odd in a building that had been with no means of heating. My exploration mood was ebbing and with thoughts of returning to the guardhouse and lighting the stove foremost in my mind, I decided to cut short a tour of the ground floor rooms and make straight for upstairs. By the time I had climbed the stairs and was standing in the main corridor, the silence had become overwhelming and again that humid close atmosphere continued to swamp the place.

I felt like an intruder as I walked around the flying control room. My footsteps were amplified by the emptiness of the place, most of the equipment and furniture had been stripped out and taken away. A crooked station clock frozen in time at 16.55 hours was left on the wall and the large operations blackboard still showing a few chalk entries for the last flying operations. I drew closer but couldn't make out the details, it had been partly wiped away, but it looked like August.

On the other wall, still in place, was an old plan of the runways showing which were in use and underneath that was an oak desk and chair. Another table stood underneath the front windows and on it came the most poignant reminders of times past - an officers cap. I walked over and studied it, but felt a hesitation at picking it up. I gave a snort and thought of some absent-minded officer leaving it behind in his haste to lock up and leave this barren place.

Exploring further I decided to exit by the side door from this room and climb the outside metal staircase to have a look on the roof with its tiny observation room. To my surprise the door wasn't locked, maybe the same absent-minded officer had been at work again. The wind buffeted me as I climbed the stairs, but I didn't mind in fact it was welcome after the stuffy silence inside. I stood with my hands on the pitted railings looking out over the forlorn runways and dispersals, then I turned and looked back at the dark hangars with the wind in my face. Entering the battered glasshouse had been easy as it also hadn't been locked. It was empty except for a pair of rustic binoculars which I put to effective use.

What a joyless and featureless place this was, the black trees that skirted the far edges of the site looked even more sinister and suggestive now. I returned the antique binoculars and made my way back to the flying control room. Once back in the time frozen control room, I had the uneasy feeling that during my brief absence something evil had entered the room. The closeness was still present but now something more malign lingered. The light caught recently disturbed dust floating lazily and I found myself drawn to the officer's cap - it seemed to me it was now laying at a different angle - there was a repugnance about the relic.

I was brought out of my unhealthy deliberations with a start. The heated silence was momentarily shattered by a door slamming apparently from downstairs. Then nothing, I waited, then came a few crisp footsteps, I still waited - nothing. I called out "Hello who's there?" The reply I got, if one can call it that, made me think about the very real idea of exiting the building by jumping from the balcony! It was a short burst of something unintelligible delivered in a preternatural monotone voice swamped in static. I stood rooted to the spot, fists clenched, hairs raised on my neck, praying the abnormal sound would not come again. Silence once again returned but with an even more tainted unwholesome air. I wanted to leave this muggy imprisonment but that would mean the stairs and moving closer to whatever made that terrifying sound in answer to my call. Had something beyond my comprehension taken up residence in the disused Control Tower? Was I in actual danger? What if it started to climb the stairs? Then what? If it looked as other-worldly as the sounds it made, how would I cope?

I acted almost automatically and walked into the corridor, the stairs facing me. A feverish glance to my left revealed one of the rooms had a smashed window. The cool refreshing wind which blew through the fist sized hole seemed to rouse me from my fear and analysis momentarily. In two seconds, I was on the landing and in another two I was outside the troubled building slamming the door and turning the key as flakes of paint rained down.

I put a considerable distance between myself and the Control Tower before I stole a glance back. It wasn't pity which the building invoked in me now - it was fear.

A few days after this frightening but bizarre experience the weather lifted and a cheery October sun greeted me finally at Woodlands. The soaking runways started to dry in patches and in places steam rose. The blue sky breathed a fresh look into my world. Gone was the oppressive feeling. By midday a heat shimmer was visible as I stared out across the flat vastness. I had once again locked the barrier (by now the base was being used for the already mentioned training) and while putting the usual check call through, I was told to cycle over to the main accommodation block and report its condition and conduct a feasibility study as to it possible reuse.

I had resurrected the long-forgotten rusty bicycle and was soon peddling down the main runway with the sun on my back and wind in hair. Dozens of tyre marks were still visible on the degrading concrete, sometimes suggesting a very precarious landing some even lurched of the centre line and left the concrete altogether. Soon I reached the end and parked up on the perimeter track looking back across the site. The sun glinted from the little observation room perched on top of the sinister Control Tower and grass swayed gently all around. Next, I followed the perimeter track a short distance then turned off and followed a track across a field and then into the start of the forest. I was working on memory from a layout of the airfield back at the Guard Room.

Once under the canopies, the suns beating charm left me, and an unwelcome damp feeling consumed all. The familiar latrine, ablutions and drying blocks came into view and then came the barrack huts dotted all around. They were the standard Nissan huts – 9024/41 with a dimension of 16ft x 36 ft. Further on I could make out the Airmen's barrack blocks of a different design – 5150/40. The place looked more like a medieval encampment.

The trees towered over the diminutive buildings and in places brushed the windows with skeletal leafy arms. Ferns and bracken were strewn about in unsightly clumps, waiting to trip the unwary. Sunlight broke through in thin weedy rays and ricocheted off the tin roofs fast becoming streaked with rust and mould. The whole area looked foreboding and seemed to produce a depressing atmosphere. Gingerly I stalked thoughtfully about the grounds and balked at the idea of anyone spending a night here, let alone making one of the staring cold huts their new accommodation. Having decided that this dankness would hardly be conducive to a good night's rest, what with the air having to compete with all the damp branches and the smell of mould always on the wind, I fashioned a plan as I continued my tour. I would simply say the site was too run down and recommend billets be set up in one of the many buildings closer to the tower and hangars.

For all the world I felt like the last person in existence as I shuffled round this sinister sleepy hollow occasionally stopping to clean a window and look through at the emptiness. I was on the point of heading back to the main path and finding the tired bicycle, when one of the less weathered Nissan huts caught my eye. It stood a little apart from the rest, and the peeling door swung idly open every so often tapping shut and then creaking back in a gentle sway.

Against my better judgment and with the Control Tower drama still swirling round in my mind, I found myself drawn to investigate and before I knew much more about it, I had pushed the door back and was inside the empty structure.

The stove in the centre of the room was of course familiar to me, but other than that the room was gutted and featureless. But wait, on the opposite wall under a few years of dust and black mould the room revealed its melancholy secret. Dozens of hand drawn pictures and messages left by the previous residents. Everything from the crude and simple to highly skilled cartoon pictures and murals. Many depicting Germany being bombed and Hitler getting a boot up the arse, and some were simply a name and the duration of their stay. I noted with no surprise, and almost at the same time a chill passed over me, that many of the writings had expressed a deep loathing for the base and a longing to leave.

One well executed drawing that was closest to the corner of the room, depicted six, four engine bombers flying low as if to land. The Control Tower was in the foreground but behind the aircraft a huge formation of cloud or fog looking as if to engulf them. As I stared longer, I realised that the creator of this forgotten artwork had been very clever indeed. The longer you stared at it or into it, you became aware of what was looking back at you in plain sight. The cloud formation was that of an enormous skull with empty eye sockets and a slight grin made up of smaller clouds. It seemed to be gloating over the doomed aircraft waiting for them to fall to earth. The effect was as frightening as it was artistic. The piece was chillingly called "The Usual Woodlands Welcome". I closed my eyes and turned my head but still the skull was burnt into my mind and remained, only leaving me when I had left the building.

I regained the path then the perimeter track and once again felt the sun on my back and a freshness that I had been without since entering the festering ill-omened accommodation site.

After these events, when on duty, I tried at all costs to stay rooted to the Guard Room only venturing out if it was absolutely necessary. There was a calamitous and malevolent atmosphere about the whole place, it was as if something was always waiting for you to be at your most vulnerable.

One afternoon a colleague paid me a visit, I had to go to enormous lengths to conceal my relief at his company or else he might think me odd. After a pot of tea, he suggested a patrol round to which I replied "It's all very boring trust me". But he would hear none of it and off we set. We must have been gone over 30 minutes when the weather turned and a slight drizzle became a down-pour. While looking over buildings on the technical site the rain then worsened to the extent that we found ourselves taking impromptu shelter in the parachute stores building- type 17865/39. The building was easily identified by the design of the roof and once inside we could do nothing but smoke and wait for the swish of the rain to abate.

The place was a gutted shell and offered nothing to distract us. After some 15 minutes of silent pacing about we heard or thought we heard muffled voices some way off.

Assuming more colleagues had arrived and found the main gate unmanned and were now looking for us perhaps not in the best of moods - we decided to exit our shelter and make a dash back to the guardhouse. But what was this? The fog…in the 15 short minutes we had been inside the area had become alien to us enveloped in swirling fog. Visibility was down to 20 feet at best.

We made the journey back in total silence groping and tripping like blind men. At last we found the perimeter track and would follow this until the hangars and Control Tower came into view. It was on my mind and I'm sure my friends also as to how could a fog so unnervingly dense as this descend so quickly and compressively? It twisted and writhed all around us, deadened all sound as if in a vacuum. To me it felt like some unknown agent wanted us stranded out there, somehow alone in time and space.

Eventually the all-seeing Control Tower came into sight with its sombre windows offering the best welcome it could. We hurried back to the Guard Room and wakened the slumbering stove; the fog had brought with it an intense chill.

I was to have one more encounter or experience, call it what you will, before I was to vacate the base forever and at the time it served only wet my appetite to leave!

After a busy day I was once again seeing the last personnel off site when out of a packed transport some wag chucked a bunch of keys in my general direction and then followed this up with "I can't get the hangar doors closed, sort it for me will you mate." My heart sank. I must be honest, although it was my job to make sure all buildings that had been used were secure, I had simply been staying holed up in the guardroom and letting the cursed place get on with it. It seemed that every journey on my own seemed to bring about habitual menace

I made my way timorously over in the growing dusk to the two massive hangars. These were standard T2'S type- 825/40. There was also one B1 type – 11776/41. The nearest hangar wasn't supposed to be in use but I was disheartened to find that it had also been left open. I squeezed through the doors, and found the smell of dirty oil hung in the air of the cavernous interior. I walked round surveying the scene, the far end was strewn with engine parts and smaller sections of plane fuselage. Birds flapped above me and darted about in the rusty lattice work of the roof structure. Water dripped down in random places leaving dark green pools scattered about on the floor. The abandonment was complete. I squeezed back through the doors and closed them having seen enough.

The second hangar doors were jammed open leaving a gap of about 4 feet. I once again surveyed the impressive vastness. No dissected aircraft parts or plucked engine assortments this time just a few well stacked tyres in one corner. My footsteps echoed off the vast walls in a hollow sounding pitch as I walked to the other end of the building to secure a side door. With this done I quickly made my way back to the jammed doors. A few feet from the door I stopped and found myself glancing back at the emptiness inside. The feeling of being watched suddenly came over me - but the place was empty, there simply was nothing there, just floor space and towering walls. The feeling came again, not so much watched anymore but scrutinised in a mocking way. How or why I picked up on this I'm at a loss to explain, there was nothing in the hangar to give rise to such feelings.

If my time at Woodlands has taught me anything it's that you don't linger when that feeling comes over you. I had no intention of wrestling anymore with the stuck doors and would report them as a maintenance issue. Just then I heard the sound of a radial engine being run up from inside the empty hangar - it was unmistakable! I felt nervous to say the least and wasn't about to go dashing in to investigate. I stole a quick glance through the gap in the doors as the din continued. Left and right of the building were in darkness the only light being afforded was from a shaft the jammed door let into the vastness.

Figures were walking in and out of the light. Two

figures seem to be in some sort of frantic activity. Just then the engine noise ceased and so too did the perambulations of the figures.

Without question it was two men wearing Sidcot suits (old flying suits) they seemed to be a drab olive colour. I dropped the keys to the ground in terror, the two "men" turned at once in my direction and to my absolute horror revealed that neither had a face. I was quite literally watching empty suits complete with full flying helmet - the left figure had goggles but both were devoid of a face or any features. The two marionettes seem to bob and sway several times adding more disbelief to their awful appearance. Gaining tremendous strength through fear, I managed to pull the hangar door closed a little and quickly made my way back to the safety of the old Guard Room.

I spent the rest of my shift barricaded in my quarters, stove glowing and radio on. The wind rattled the door every so often as if to test my resolve, and all my glances out the window were met with a sickly green glow emanating from the empty Control Tower.

Finally, some long overdue luck came my way and it transpired that this would be the last time I would have to endure the phantoms of the Woodlands base. I was posted back to my airfield the following day and a new group of unfortunates arrived to have their outlooks broadened.

The airfield closed altogether three months later and the site was quickly returned to agriculture and soon became amalgamated spectres within the Norfolk countryside.

Only the brooding skeletal Control Tower remains to keep a lookout over what used to be. Many a person has entered its gaunt shell out of idle curiosity, and many a person has fled across the fields and never looked back.

"CARE" AND KILLING

"Any benevolent organisation no matter how well intentioned isn't without its own personal monsters and parasites. As in nature the weakest suffer first and offer easy pickings. The saying absolute power corrupts absolutely is a truthfully sad indictment. People without a conscience are all sound sleepers."

Bayview Nursing Home the South of England 1985.

A tall thin blue uniformed woman is helping a resident elderly lady out of a fireside chair. Things seem fraught. The resident is resisting and complaining, her gnarled fingers struggling to grip the walking frame. "Take the frame, take the frame. Don't act up!" the uniformed women barks viciously. The elderly resident's feeble efforts finally result in both her hands desperately clinging to the walking frame and when at last composed, she asks "Must you be so rude?"

The sweeping kick the tall uniformed woman (I won't say lady) delivered, takes the frame right out from underneath the defenceless resident and had the intended effect of delivering her to the floor in seconds with a sound denoting extreme frailty. "Staff, staff! I need help Mrs Daniels has fallen over again."

Welcome to the domain of senior care supervisor Christine Mayfield. A thief, bully, abuser and murderess. A human being happy to take money from her fellow kind and offer soothing words of comfort to bereaved relatives while hiding under a thin veneer of respectability.

Bayview care home was opened in 1979 and occupied a large Victorian mansion. The house had once been owned by a very wealthy brewing family and used as their headquarters; it was only relinquished when the company was bought out. The current owner had no use for the large house but did not want to sell it, so it was agreed with the local authority that it could be converted to a care home and a peppercorn rent charged.

77

Mayfield joined the care home right from its conception and finally rose to senior care supervisor in 1983 to the exclusion and fear of all others. She was in her early 50s slim, tall at 5'10, very short greying hair with a rather severe fringe, piecing grey eyes and thin lips and nose. She had never married and when asked about romantic interests would reply "I'm married to my care duties." Her position entitled her to a one-bedroom apartment located at the top of the mansion in the one-time servants' rooms. This she told colleagues was an extra bonus as it meant she could be 'on hand anytime if there's trouble'. Mayfield seldom indulged in cultural pursuits that took her away from Bayview, so her feared controlling presence cast an ominous shadow even on her days off.

Most decent, thoughtful and compassionate people look upon the horrors of Nazi Germany with shame and disgust, this was, I am saddened to say, not the case with senior care supervisor Mayfield.

One thing that fascinated and impressed her was how the Nazis dealt with people they classed as 'undesirables' during World War 2. It was the way this brutal regime was able to "process" people that she admired the most. Her findings showed how an inmate could be assessed, segregated, stripped of their life's worth and then either disposed of immediately or used as a commodity until the inevitable end result.

Mayfield was able to conceal her crimes at Bayview by putting her found knowledge to appalling use, she was very careful how, and who she 'picked for processing'.

Rich inmates, sorry I mean residents, went to the top of her list for 'special treatment'. This had to be done carefully though…. an obviously wealthy resident was a danger if they had a large family and regular visits. Too many questions would be asked if little keep sakes went missing. However, and most cowedly of all, a wealthy resident showing signs of senility, with little in the way of family was a delight for Mayfield. Such people (male or female) were systematically robbed of jewellery over a period of a few months.

At any time, a resident could be victim to a nasty fall, and should a concerned or upset relative ask questions, Mayfield delivered her standard pattern line over porcelain tea cups. "They will wonder about, we have 40 residents to watch over, it's not as though we can strap them to bed that would be inhumane."

There was the case of Gittings, a retired Colonel in his 80's but of sound mind. He was scheduled for only a short stay at Bayview while his warden controlled flat was being updated. The stay unfortunately was forever. Mayfield had assessed Col Gittings in her to "be left alone" category, large family, too many friends and only a short stay. The one mistake he made, which signed his death certificate, was to pull out a solid gold Edwardian half hunter watch and politely give the time to a fellow resident when asked. The evil magpie greedily eyed this gold trinket and decided to break her own processing rules.

Colonel Gittings was harangued on a daily basis by the odious fiend about the dangers of having such a high value item about his person. "It will get taken, they wonder about and steal things, we won't be held responsible", she would tell him. But Colonel Gittings would hear none of it and said the watch had belonged to his father and had never left his side in 40 years.

One night after dinner, as he climbed the stairs to his room, Mayfield stopped him and when the usual nagging drew a blank yet again, the old man snapped back at her impatiently - "I think you want it for yourself" he exploded. Mayfield's minuscule layer of respectability suddenly evaporated and was replaced by a fuming bullying monster, red in the face with glaring eyes.

"You've had your chance, your old fool" she shouted in his face and without any provocation pushed him clean over the banisters and down the sweeping staircase.

"Staff, staff, Colonel Gittings has had a fall." The workforce was quickly mobilised, one person to call an ambulance, the others to check the other residents. Mayfield, under the shambolic act of delivering first aid, slipped her hand into Colonel Gittings blood stained waistcoat and removed the golden relic.

The grieving relatives of Colonel Gittings did enquire about his watch but were informed how the nice care supervisor had asked him time and time again to leave it in the office safe as the other more confused residents have a habit of taking belongings.

And what became of the two antique cameo broches of Miss Stevens? The gold bracelet of Mrs Bartlett? Or the expensive stamp collection that the widow Simpson would happily pour over in her favourite chair? All mysteriously mislaid...

A disused service elevator that had once been used to carry heavy kegs and barrels provided another means to terrorise the helpless residents. This was pressed into service as a macabre version of solitary confinement. Poor senile Mr Booth and been locked in this place of torment until he surrendered his late wife Pearl's drop earrings and other cherished items that he kept to aid his failing memory. When Mr Booth did go on to join the death list at Bayview his eldest daughter was treated to a really first-rate performance of the standard patter line "we have 40 residents "etc.

A subject for considerable conjecture is how much, if anything, the other staff knew of the tyrannical Mayfield. This appalling woman was their immediate boss and in total charge of the home in the general managers absentia. It is worth pointing out that Bayview had a fairly high turnover of staff in proportion to other care homes in the county. It could well have been that Mayfield had assessed which staff would 'turn a blind eye' or go along with her regime. Others who threatened her empire could be transferred of sacked on a pretext.

Two new arrivals in late September were quickly assessed by Mayfield in her honed to perfection system. Miss Adams: no valuables other than table and chairs (residents were allowed to furnish their own rooms) regular visits from the local vicar and a daughter working for the town council. Of no interest.

The other new target promised much better pickings. A Mrs Mendez originally from Spain but travelled widely. She was 80 but still retained natural dark hair, average build but little more than 5ft in height and usually wore dark clothes. Mrs Mendez was a much-loved chatterbox always regaling staff and residents alike with fascinating tales of her travels. She was polite and friendly and although always had a story to fit any occasion, never out stayed her welcome.

Mayfield loathed the woman, she hated the attention and respect she got, she hated her knowledge and hated the fact she seemed to boost morale in her 'camp'. The tyrant found it hard to control her jealousy and rage around Mendez, it was only the fact that Mendez had no living relatives and had several items of interest that she tolerated her.

Apart from selected jewellery in a musical box which could be picked over at a later date and the loss blamed on other residents, what had really caught the thief's eye was a striking necklace and medallion that Mendez wore every day. It was a chunky silver chain and on it hung a huge carved red stone. Mrs Mendez had said it was a ruby, and this extraordinary stone had silver snakes coiled and intertwined round it. One snake had an open mouth and forked tongue while the other snake's mouth was closed but with staring eyes. The stone itself had an iridescent quality about it that was almost hypnotic.

Mayfield eyed Mrs Mendez with indignation as the

unsuspecting victim sat eating her meal one evening, the red stone prominently displayed on her black blouse.

I must have that for my collection! Even if I have to smother you. I'll try the Gittings watch routine and if that doesn't work maybe a spell in confinement will cool your jabber, she thought.

"Something wrong supervisor?" a member of staff asked. Mayfield spun around "No of course not, just seeing all was ok before I went off shift. Tell me, that Mrs Mendez, how is she behaving?"

"Oh, she's no trouble at all. The stories she tells and some of the places she's been to! I could talk to her for hours. Some of it is a bit weird I must say but so interesting."

Mayfield stalked off after this exchange and headed for her apartment.

About two months after her arrival Mrs Mendez learnt the true horror of Bayview when Mayfield, having grown bored of being pleasant to her decided to launch a decisive attack.

Mayfield quietly entered the large sitting room, finding Mrs Mendez all alone and busy with her cross stitch. She softly closed the door behind her. Her tall frame towered over the diminutive old lady. "Put that down and listen!" she said in a sharp piecing tone. Mrs Mendez reacted with a start but before she could reply Mayfield continued the ambush.

"I run Bayview, me!! I don't like you, who do you think you are? Who said you could tell stories? I'm reporting you as a disruptive influence at once. You will be sent to a dirty tower block or something, no grounds to walk in and no ornate rooms like here."

Mrs Mendez went to get up but the towering omen above her, pushed her back down into the depths of the chair and kept her there with one long hand on her shoulder, then kneeled beside her and whispered in her ear. "You're nothing, just a commodity. I'm always here and always will be. You, and people like you come and go. I choose how long they stay…me! You might be leaving in a rubber bag by next week, I haven't decided yet."

The old lady burst into to tears and whimpered "Don't send me away, I've made friends, what can I do? What can I do?", she begged.

"Give me the medallion now! You will only lose it anyway - you daft old bag."

"I can't it's got a malediction or something if you…."

"SHUT UP," interrupted Mayfield - not prepared to stop now.

"Are you sure you want it?" cried Mrs Mendez

"Hand it over I won't tell you again, don't push your luck," Mayfield retorted.

"Take it and what comes with it," Mendez sobbed and placed it in the palm of Mayfield's sweaty grasping hand.

"Now wipe your snotty nose and keep your mouth shut, this is only the start. One word and your feet won't touch," Mayfield replied.

Like some kind of beast that retreats to a corner to devour a side of meat, Mayfield scurried away from the degrading scene and retired to her apartment. Large vodka in hand and humming a ditty of satisfaction, the victor cast her mean eye over the spoils. It was unlike anything she had seen or 'confiscated' before. The engraving work on the snakes was unapparelled, and intricate to the point of obsessive in its detail. The stone was even more exquisite close up, totally flawless and a deep rich red. Next, she tried on her latest acquisition and studied herself in a full-length mirror. The effect was pleasing to her and produced an almost Junoesque quality. After strutting about for a few minutes, she bent down and produced an old green cash box from underneath the sofa.

Once opened, it revealed her treasure trove of ill-gotten gains. It was more than half full of jewellery, she took off the medallion and stared into the dark red sheen. "At least I appreciate it, with her it would only be pearls before swine", she muttered to herself. She gently placed the stone and chain on the top of this sinister collection and then carefully replaced the box. Not long afterwards she began to feel drowsy and gave in to a feverish desire to sleep.

Waking on the sofa with a thumping headache and feeling nauseous at around 2am, Mayfield struggled to fathom the reason for her sudden indisposition. She reasoned it couldn't have been the drink as she only had one. The room span and seemed in a state of flux. After some minutes the nausea subsided and she managed to partly shrug off some of the lassitude, the coldness in the room was unusual and it hastened her desire to go to bed.

As she doddered into the little corridor that led to her tiny staircase, it became apparent the hallway light was on. This was odd as the light in question was similar to those found in student accommodation or shared dorms, once pressed in would stay on for 20 seconds or so to allow the person to climb the stairs safely. She placed her foot on the first of the carpeted stairs, they angled round sharply before the main steep stairs began. Looking down, the narrow stairs revealed themselves to be quite empty. The view didn't allow all the stairs to be seen, they veered off to the right and another 4 or 5 steps were out of site before coming to the entrance/exit door. She thought it odd, but with that the light went out and she was left staring down into the darkness.

A little while later, and now in bed in the attitude of sleep, an idle glance at the gap under the door showed a strip of light. Again, a journey to the stairs revealed the area to be empty... The idea of descending the stairs and looking around the corner did cross her mind but something stopped her. The light once again went out and a chill accompanied the darkness this time. Back turned, and on the point of leaving when she heard the familiar 'click' of the stair light and was once again aware of the dim light now being on again...

While holding onto the banister she leaned round and cast a tremulous look down the narrow stairway. This time however the shadowy bottom stairs were now occupied by a towering wraith like figure in some kind of blood red gown. Dark hair came past its shoulders and half covered a deathly pale face with sunken features. Two piercing elliptical nefarious yellow eyes stared out from the black hair with a blasphemous coldness. Hands and wrists were visible from beneath the sanguine garment, they were both horribly pink and blistered as if freshy burnt.

Once again, a drowsiness enveloped Mayfield, her eyes began to drift in and out of focus. This, combined with the poor lighting, made her last words spoken on earth a fitting testament to what a truly ignorant poor example of a human being she had become. "Get back to your bed! How dare you disturb me. You'll get a beating for this." The figure remained reticent, and then as if moving in-between time had advanced onto the next step but seemingly without moving and then it appeared on the next and the next...

. . . .

"It's a terrible mess isn't it gov?" said DC Jones.

"Yes, Jones you don't have to keep saying it!" The scene of crimes officer has already been sick twice"

Inspector Wynn surveyed the apartment and consulted the note book of DC Jones and scratched his chin. "Hmmm"

They were right to be baffled and disgusted because

Christine Mayfield had met a truly catastrophic demise. She was found after two male orderlies were asked to break down the door to her apartment after having missed two shifts in a row. The spectacle that had greeted them all but destroyed their sanity. The remains of Mayfield where to be found on the sofa, not bundled but neatly placed. This same sofa had become a make shift operating table as the attacker performed diabolical "procedures" long into and after death agony.

Inspector Wynn summed it up most descriptively by saying her that her face 'looked like one of those baroque Egyptian tomb figures'.

The late Col Gittings' gold pocket watch had been shoved into her mouth with enough force to break several teeth. Mrs Bartlett's bracelet had been surgically detached into three equal sections, two had been pressed in a downward attitude on her eyebrows with such strength they now sat several millimetres below the surface and simulated a frown. The third section had been crushed onto the nose with equal force causing considerable mess and finished off with a flared nostril look courtesy of Mr Booths late wife's pearl earrings. Miss Stevens' two cameo broches had found a new home as replacement eyes on Mayfield's corpse, having been pushed into place with the utmost care. The whole effect was completed by the face having been decorated with the widow Simpsons' stamp collection.

A corners inquest was held due to the suddenness and unexplained nature of death. Inspector Wynn submitted comprehensive details such as the ground floor entrance to the apartment being locked from the inside. All the windows were also fastened from the inside and entrance to the top apartment was ruled out as impossible by means of climbing. All of the jewellery and the other items in the cash box that had decorated Mayfield's body, were identified as having belonged to former residents and this exposed her revolting side-line and exploitation.

A ruling of unlawful killing was pronounced and people did their best to forgot about the name Christine Mayfield.

Two months after the inquest three members of staff quietly entered the sitting room of Bayview and close the door behind them. Mrs Mendez was sitting alone dozing in the sunshine that floods in through the huge bay windows making the parquet floor appear bright orange.

"Mrs Mendez" one calls softy.

"Oh, hello loves I didn't hear you come in" She replied.

"We just wanted to give you this back now all the fuss has died down."

The youngest of the three took out the red stoned medallion with its watchful serpents and places it gently into her wizened hand.

Mrs Mendez smiled, "It usually does the trick if you relinquish it correctly. I was given it in Haiti on my travels many years ago now. I made sure I wore it at all times like you suggested. Thank you for returning it girls"

"No, it's all of us who should thank you Mrs Mendez. If it hadn't been for all your tales of travelling and strange experiences and talk of hexes, we might never have come up with a way to get rid of her.

You see, there was only one group of people who hated her more than the residents and that was the staff.

After general chit chat one of them attempted to ask "But how does it..."

Mrs Mendez politely interrupted. "It doesn't do to question providence dear; some things are better left unexplained."

"It doesn't take much to strip a person of their dignity, take their possessions, oversee the daily aspects of their lives and ultimately treat them like an expendable asset. The more vulnerable the victim the easier it becomes. But abuser be warned, sooner or later people of this kind all meet their Waterloo.

THE LESSER KNOWN EXPERIMENT

The more things change, the more they stay the same. The boundaries of science are pushed beyond our understanding, not for the benefit of mankind and charity but simply to get the drop on one's enemy. Maybe it was this very motive that brought about a judgement...

I'm sure that many of you have heard of a dubious experiment that our cousins across the water allegedly conducted in 1943 and yielded disastrous results. The name of this experiment is widely known and attracts a large number of believers and sceptics alike. Here is just a brief recap for those not conversant with this work.

The United States military desire was to render a craft (in this case a destroyer) invisible or cloaked to radar and other enemy devices. The generally accepted story is that generators installed onboard the ship were used to create an intense magnetic field. This would cause refraction or bending of light and radar waves around the ship. The disastrous result was that the ship actually disappeared altogether for a period of time, supposedly travelled in time, and appeared elsewhere. Upon its return the crew were discovered in varying states of health.

As I have stated, this is all very widely known, so now let me tell you about a similar experiment that was conducted some years later after this allegedly happened and has escaped such recognition and fame.

The United Kingdom 1956

The experiment was a joint RAF/ Navy venture for a number of reasons. Obviously, a joint venture would mean a greater budget and more available facilities, but more importantly if the initial series of test proved successful it could be applied equally to both services - combat, ships and planes.

I suppose one could best describe this as an early

attempt at "stealth fighter" technology, which is readily available nowadays in certain countries arsenals. A large passenger sized aircraft would be secretly flown to a designated airbase where it would have equipment installed and undergo ground tests before the next stage of airborne testing commenced. If all went well, further experiments would be signed off as phase 2, but only if there was good cause to continue. It was not only being monitored by high ranking military but security cleared civil servants reporting directly to the Minister for Defence.

The V bombers were being introduced in and around this time (Vulcan introduced 1956, Victor 1958). Therefore, if a large aircraft could somehow be made invisible to enemy radar even for a short period it would prove a huge tactical advantage.

The selected aircraft was a Bristol Britannia, these had their first flight in 1952 and introduced in 1957 with a small production run numbering 85.

The Britannia's were manufactured by the Bristol Aeroplane Company, powered by four Bristol Proteus 755 turboprops. Although I can't be sure of the exact variant used for the tests the dimensions are: wing span 43.36 meters, length 37.87 meters, height 11.43 meters and with a total wing area of 192.8 meters.

The aircraft arrived brand new at an airbase in Gloucestershire in the summer of 1956. It was comprehensively looked over and stripped out. Then three weeks were spent installing three large generators, magnetic coils were secured underneath the fuselage and other equipment such as transmitters and amplifiers etc were all crammed inside. A further two weeks was then allotted to ground testing and obtaining baseline readings.

Finally, the first airborne test was given the go ahead and take off would be the 14th of August.

The handpicked flight deck crew consisted of, Captain, First Officer, Navigator and Radio Operator, while in the rear of the plane there would be two civilian engineers operating the installed equipment. Making a total compliment of six.

The Bristol Britannia took off at exactly 09.00 hours like a whispering giant and in excellent weather conditions. The aircraft was held in circuit for 20 minutes while some adjustments and a slight malfunction were corrected and cleared to proceed with its flight plan. The main tests would be conducted over the Celtic sea to minimise collateral damage in case of a serious problem resulting in a bale out. Two Royal Naval ships were to be in the area tracking the Britannia. For a visual observation, an Avro Shackleton would meet up with the aircraft over the Bristol Channel, and would be filming throughout all the tests.

Once in position, permission was given to commence and several tests were conducted, - high altitude, low altitude, different speeds etc - then more settings were changed and calculations made. The power being tapped from the engines to run the generators was alarmingly prodigious. However, the desired result of masking the plane from radar even partially was proving a wash-out. Data was constantly monitored and relayed back to mission control in Gloucestershire.

Satisfied that the equipment was operating within expected tolerances and with time growing short, the go ahead was given to increase power to all generators to full.

It was the crew of the Shackleton who were the first to notice anything out of the ordinary. The Britannia suddenly adopted a brilliant blue outline, much brighter than the clear skies that surrounded it. The effect was like someone having drawn around it with a bright marker pen. This phenomenon was reported back to control immediately. At this time radio contact was lost with the crew of the Britannia.

The blue outline was becoming brighter but the aircraft was perfectly clear and what's more the naval ships still reported it showing on radar.

Seconds ticked away, the crew of the Shackleton could do nothing; the blue outline was now too bright to look at directly and they had to avert their gaze. They were constantly reminded to keep filming, and not to lose contact. An uneasy feeling was growing, any second, they expected the Britannia to break up and plummet into the cold Celtic sea. Suddenly the outline faded slightly but still remained as if glued to the aircraft, then just in front of the nose a second outline started to form.

This second materialisation didn't share the same appearance as the one holding fast around the aircraft. It was pale yellow and had the consistency of smoke. In fact, when it had grown to a massive circumference that's exactly what it resembled - a giant smoke ring!

This second appearance was clearly visible for seven or eight seconds. It matched the airspeed of the Britannia and was roughly 25 feet from the nose of the aircraft.

As if experiencing a dreadful premonition, the crew of the Shackleton continued to re-establish contact with the Britannia. They couldn't understand why the pilot had not reacted to the intimidating shape forming directly in front of them. They must surely be aware of it even if ignorant of the blue outline clinging to the contours of their plane. Instructions were explicit from control, do not break formation or interfere with the test, this again was made clear to them when they reported this new development. But before anymore calculations, observations and consternations could be cogitated the inexplicable happened.

The most detailed account is often the most basic and for this we must thank the crew of the Shackleton. To quote the pilot directly.

"The giant yellowish ring has stopped dead, but not changed its position. The Britannia has flown straight into it, and as soon as it passed the threshold of the ring-like appearance - the aircraft has disappeared totally from sight."

For exactly four seconds the Bristol Britannia vanished from all visual observation, and for exactly the same amount of allotted time the naval ships had also lost all contact.

So, what happened next? And had the experiment been a success?

The aircraft did not blow up, disintegrate or anything so dramatic. It benignly but instantly reappeared and after a brief confusion regarding watches having stopped and a slight mysterious upset with the onboard radio, contact was re-established. Orders were then received to head back to the airbase in Gloucestershire.

The huge Britannia made a perfect landing, as it taxied towards the hangars, the First Officer had requested an ambulance to stand by. At this point there was no immediate course for concern, but things would however start to take a more terrifying turn.

The emergency de-briefing that followed 30 minutes after the Britannia touched down proved to be somewhat of a damp squib. It was quickly established that all of the flight deck crew remembered very little, with the exception of Hanworth the Radio Operator. He was the recipient of the ambulance and had been stretchered off the plane unconscious and was yet to wake.

The Captain, First Officer and Navigator could only remember events up to the loss of radio contact. After that they had no recollection of anything else until (unbeknown to them) the aircraft reappeared and they were instructed to return to base.

The two civilian engineers in the rear of the aircraft who had been operating the equipment could remember even less - both of their accounts tallied, and their last memory was of turning all generators up to maximum power.

Now, about the Radio Operator Hanworth, he had been found in the rear of the aircraft by the two engineers at the moment the aircraft was ordered to return, he was unconscious, and his breathing shallow. No one onboard could remember or had any recollection of Hanworth leaving his seat and going to the rear of the airplane, and no one could offer a reason why he would want to. I should point out that the crew of the Britannia were not told what had happened for those four seconds at this point.

The next logical step by officials was to examine the physical evidence and data, this was irrefutable and did not rely on human memory.

The Royal Naval ships radar tracking data confirmed the eye witness reports from the crew of the Shackleton. The blip of the Britannia had indeed disappeared for four seconds from their screens. This at least alleviated the shadow of human error but also proved baffling.

I said earlier the Shackleton crew were filming the Britannia in addition to making visual observations. So, it was with a zealous impatience that officials waited for the film to be developed and rushed to them.

The Shackleton had been ordered not to return to its own base but return and land with the Britannia and maintain observation. The moment it touched down the film had been spirited away to the technical site to be processed. A projector screen had been hastily erected in the corner of the oak panelled meeting room. There was an urgent gasp of disbelief in the smoke-filled room, as the selected officials witnessed the unbelievable! The crew of the Shackleton version of events was collaborated by the film footage they shot at the time in unnerving accuracy.

An Air Commodore spoke for everyone when looking over the footage for the second time (shot in colour) and uttered the words "it is the damnedest thing". A few other officials looked at one another, each hoping the person next to him could offer a logical explanation, and all the while sharing a common thought "what exactly have we done?"

It was almost like a conjuring trick, at first all seemed normal. Then a very vivid blue outline appeared around the aircraft, growing brighter ten seconds after it first appeared. At this point the blue outline pulsated slightly and became so bright the camera could not focus on the subject. The footage became shaky as the crewman struggled to avert his eyes.

After eight seconds this intense brightness suddenly grew dimmer and the cameraman was able to lock back on to the Britannia, which remained undamaged and not in difficulty.

Three seconds after this, a second outline, much paler in colour, appeared immediately in front of the Britannia and matched its airspeed. This second appearance, manifestation, call it what you will, had a wispy cloud like resemblance, it soon grew into a huge ring shape.

Eight seconds after it first became visible this second phenomenon appeared to stop dead, or maybe it accelerated towards the Britannia - it was quite impossible to tell. At this point the Britannia disappeared into its centre and vanished.

When slowed down the film revealed the aircraft disappearing inch by inch as it entered the ring. The split second the tail disappeared; the colossal ring then disappeared instantaneously. Precisely four seconds elapsed and the Britannia re-appeared, with no second smoke ring or blue outline. It just appeared on the film as if spliced in - it was uncanny to say the least!

With no explanations forthcoming, orders were given to have large blow-up stills made of the key moments in the event. The Bristol Britannia was carefully manoeuvred into a hangar for close examination and a veil of secrecy descended.

Hanworth was still unavailable to give his account of events, and with the aircraft still undergoing examination, attention once again focused on interviewing the crew and civilian engineers. Time elapsed since landing three hours thirty-four minutes.

Before the Captain and First Officer could be interviewed another meeting was hastily convened, the blow-up stills were back from the dark room hardly dry. Words like "ridiculous" and "absurd" were being freely bandied about and a fidgety general discussion had spontaneously broken out. But why?

A batch of four blow ups were poured over. Photograph one showed the moment just before the Britannia entered the ominous smoke ring. Photograph two showed only the tail of the aircraft with the rest of the plane having seemingly disappeared. Photograph four showed the aircraft flying with no abnormalities.

Photograph three had grown crumpled lineaments, a testament to the amount of times it had been poured over and restudied. It showed an empty sky no Britannia or light anomalies, however upon closer examination a chilling discovery was soon made. A figure in the attitude of laying down was clearly visible in mid-air at the position the Britannia's rear fuselage would have been. This was not a figure of some unknown alien being, or unidentified person, this figure was undeniably that of the Radio Operator Hanworth.

For a brief moment in time, against all the laws of physics Hanworth was outside the aeroplane but yet still remained in his relative fixed position, exactly as he had been found by the ground and ambulance crew.

This last development served only to increase the hysteria. Hanworth was still unconscious. The aircraft hadn't given up any secrets yet, so the only remaining option left was to go over events with the Captain and First Officer of both aircraft, starting with the Britannia.

However, any chance of ever talking to the flight deck crew of the Britannia were quickly lost at around four hours forty-six minutes after landing and events descended from the unbelievable to the nightmarish.

101

The Captain and First Officer had not shown up for the second debriefing, a search of their quarters, the mess and all other likely places had drawn a blank.

Then came the ghoulish discovery of two RAF uniforms in the scheduled debriefing room. No one had noticed these at first as they were under a large table and partly on two chairs that had been pulled out, as a chair would be if occupied. What had happened to them? The uniforms undoubtedly belonged to them. The evidence pointed to them having arrived on time for the second debriefing. They had been told to wait as it had been delayed due to discovery of the evidence on the still photographs. And sometime immediately after this they both apparently vanished, leaving only their uniforms behind. In the absence of any reports regarding two semi-nude men trying to leave the base (such an occurrence would hopefully be remembered), the time of their disappearance was fixed at the time the debriefing was originally planned to start. Another victim was soon to follow.

The Navigator's vanishing occurred in the mess but this time was witnessed by two other officers. Both stated independently that the man was sitting at a table when he became enveloped in a brilliant white light that seem to start at roughly chest level. In conjunction with this there was dense static sensation about the room, the light then expanded and became too bright to look at. The whole thing happened from start to finish in no more than four seconds, his uniform, pack of cigarettes and loose change were left on the chair. This dematerialisation had a profound effect on the two witnesses resulting in treatment for shock.

Officials at the base had no time to conduct anymore briefings about these nightmarish disappearances - it was incomprehensible - three men had vanished into thin air! Something had happened to the men on that plane – perhaps they had been exposed to something? They were powerless to stop this terrifying side effect.

Two groups were formed to deal with the situation. One was to immediately head over to the hangar, order everyone off the Britannia, find the two civilian engineers and escort them to the medical facilities under guard. Group two was to check on Hanworth and then carry on looking for clues or any trace of the three already missing. Go over everything possible, times, places, clothes anything at all that could shed some light on this hair-raising situation.

As it turned out the Britannia would take any secrets it may have been harbouring, with it on a journey into oblivion. The first group who arrived at the hangar were greeted with terror and pandemonium; tools lay scattered around, men were screaming while others stood rooted to the spot with horrified looks. Without warning the Britannia had disappeared into a bright light. Four people were onboard at the time, three fell to the ground when the plane left this existence, one suffered a broken ankle while the fourth disappeared with the aircraft. It later transpired this victim was one of the two engineers on the test flight. He had been helping check equipment and apparently seemed fine immediately before the incident.

The other engineer was hurriedly located in a storeroom close by and firmly escorted away from the maelstrom and in growing bewilderment rushed over to the medical centre.

He was quickly given an examination while being filmed, at this point he was barely lucid but asked for a pen and paper. Officials asked what was happening but they got little back. The broken man seemed to think that turning the generators on full had somehow caused some sort of dimensional disruption, the plane and other people no longer existed in this time.

He sobbed slightly but remained composed as he scribbled a quick note to his wife, then to a packed agonized room he vanished in a bright light. The note was later destroyed by the base commander.

In the aftermath, shock and confusion of the hangar scene no one had checked on Hanworth. As people somberly disbursed from the latest mini cataclysm the Medical Officer was approached and asked for the report on what time the unconscious man had disappeared.

"He hasn't gone anywhere and should be ok to answer questions in a few hours," the M.O managed to poleaxe everybody in the room with his reply!

If five men hadn't vanished without a trace, the scene to which Hanworth found himself in while squashed in his narrow bed, would have been quite comical. No less than eight people were shoehorned into a tiny room including a stenographer perched on is bed and a cine camera unceremoniously shoved in his face.

After a few sips of water and being calmly told to take his time and do his best to remember as much as possible Hanworth started his account.

The tests onboard were becoming quite tedious, they had done a high-altitude test then a very low pass, changed airspeed, changed course but the two civilian engineers didn't seem to be getting the results they had hoped for. Hanworth had received a radio messages giving instruction to make one more test run at 7000 feet and the generators were green lighted for maximum power.

Not long after he relayed these orders his radio stopped working completely, he could not send or receive. Suddenly there was a rumpus coming from the rear of the plane, the two engineers were calling out. At about this time the skipper of the Britannia noticed the plane didn't feel right. Hanworth was ordered to leave the dead radio for the time being and sent back to see what the shouting was about. The skipper was worried about the power drain on the engines and told him to be prepared to pull the plug. He thought that anymore power loss would put the plane in danger.

All the equipment was alive with an odd bluey coloured electricity it seemed to dance and jump about and made a weird discharging noise, and the atmosphere felt prickly. The two civilians were frantically engaged with some equipment one turned to Hanworth and shouted at him to pull the lever on number four generator and close it down now. Hanworth looked down and saw a large insulated lever at knee height, he reached down and grabbed the lever, the next thing he remembered was a huge jolt and being hurled backwards. He mentioned thinking or having the impression of an intense light but he assumed this was due to him blacking out. After more questions a dishevelled Hanworth had the news broken to him of what had befallen the plane, the rest of the flight deck crew and the two civilian engineers. Sighed lips spoke louder than words for all concerned.

How does an investigating body go about trying to solve something as unearthly as this? The answer is it didn't try too hard, more effort was put into covering up the disaster.

In the case of the vanishings themselves, they were totally localised to anything that had been on the Britannia. The flight crew all wore flight suits and changed clothes straight after the briefing, indeed the lockers of the doomed men were searched and found to be absent of these suits. Workers who had not been on the fatal flight in the Britannia simply fell to the hangar floor along with any tools and equipment that had been brought aboard after the plane landed. This even extended to engine oil being absent from a drip tray placed under the aircraft where a minor leak had been discovered. Every single item, no matter how insignificant, that was on the aircraft when it vanished for those four seconds, later disappeared from this plain of existence, with the one exception - Hanworth.

The crew had vanished in the same order as the plane

entered the anomaly. Captain and First Officer disappeared at exactly the same time, then the Navigator who was sat further back, then the civilian engineers, one going in conjunction with the Britannia, then the final victim disappeared eight minutes later, it was established he had moved to the very rear of the aircraft at the time of the incident.

Five men and an entire aircraft had vanished exactly five hours and nineteen minutes after touching down. One man survived through a freak accident. Several theories were put forward explaining this, but with the hardly surprising lack of keenness to recreate the test, meant that was as good as the military were going to get, just theories.

It was theorised that increasing the generators to full power so suddenly, had created an intensified magnetic field. The result was that the Britannia shifted in time and space for four seconds or appearing to vanish for four seconds to observers. How long passed onboard the aircraft we will never know due to all watches and clocks having stopped. The smoke ring appearance could have been a dimensional portal of some kind. Hanworth's unconscious state may have saved his life, or the other theory was that the huge electric shock he received somehow meant he was out of phase with all other objects and people and remained immune to the shift. The plane vanished, but he remained suspended in the same position, a truly alarming photograph was proof of this.

A cover-up quite easily explained both the loss of the while taking part in radar trials over the Celtic sea. One could argue this wasn't really that far removed from actual events, it was radar trials and the location matched. Who else would accept the truth? Hanworth was quietly sat on for a few years but stubbornly refused to vanish himself, much to the annoyance of the cover up fabricators I'm sure. He was given a generous pension and whole heartedly reminded of having signed the Official Secrets Act.

Dead men don't tell tales but very nearly dead ones do. Hanworth in old age and with terminal cancer finally told his incredible tale to a selected few.

Any and all further tests were immediately cancelled. Emphasis would eventually shift to radical new designs and radar defeating materials as used in stealth aircraft we are familiar with today, rather than any sort of artificially generated means. One scientist who reviewed the whole business and likened mankind's attempts to understand this particular sphere of science and adapt it for military purpose, as childlike and akin to sticking a fork in a plug socket. It was also pointed out things might have ended far worse than they did, and that this should be looked upon as a warning.

One country's search to gain the upper hand in the cold war brings about a series of routine experiments that quickly produce anything but routine results. A random event? A lucky strike? Or the infant steps to understanding time travel and other dimensions? The most qualified people to ask would be the "Britannia five" but of course their whereabouts are unknown...

MRS PRITCHARD'S GHOST

Ghost hunters, paranormal investigators or just
eccentrics, we all have a name for them and quite often
treat them with the distain we think they deserve.
Would you walk through an empty building or church
yard at night? Or maybe try to make contact with a lost
soul and help them to reach their destination? If you
wouldn't then possibly reserve your judgement on those
that do... "

"No, no Mrs Pritchard it's quite ridiculous, I won't be a party to such things," scalded Mr Haskins as he surveyed the woman over his thick rimmed tortoise shell glasses.

"May I remind you Mr Haskins that not only am I head of personnel here but a majority shareholder... oh and not to mention the small detail you always seem to forget that my father started the company," countered Mrs Pritchard.

"But, but," spluttered Mr Haskins, sporting the original furrowed brow.

"Good that's settled then I'll ask Mr Halfpenny to call this afternoon," She beamed.

"This afternoon? As soon as that? Does he not have a waiting list?" the deflated Haskins inquired.

"Oh, my dear Haskins have you not heard a word I've been saying? I've known Mr Halfpenny for years, he's a close friend. He'll soon sort this out."

It was later that sun-baked day that a sinister figure arrived outside the company of Pritchard and Ross in Wiltshire. The blackish caped appearance stood on the brown grass outside the main door and studied the large red brick building in the shimmering heat before crossing the threshold to Reception.

"Goodness, you startled me, can I help you sir?"

"Well hello there my dear," came the reply in a deep rich aged voice.

"I do have a habit of startling people, please accept my wholehearted apologies. My name is Theodore Halfpenny I have an appointment with Mrs Pritchard."

Mrs Pritchard who had evidently been lurking on the stairs suddenly called down "It's ok Julie I'm here, I'll deal with this. Theo my love it's so good of you to call at short notice, please come up to my office and I'll tell you all about it."

The lumbering frame of Theodore Halfpenny slowly squeaked and traversed the shiny stairs, he was well over six feet tall, in his late 60's with a thick crop of dark grey hair and in possession of a beard that would make father Christmas's look like bum fluff in comparison.

"Good god who are you?" A startled Mr Haskins whimpered as the black phantom like proportions of Mr Halfpenny entered the personnel office.

Mrs Pritchard intervened before poor Haskins either fainted or handed over his wallet in perturbation.

"This is my friend Mr Theodore Halfpenny," she proudly announced.

Over steaming cups of vending machine tea Mrs Pritchard explained her story to Halfpenny who sat silently listening. His spade like hand made the paper cup look tiny.

It transpired that yesterday evening (Thursday) Mrs Pritchard unexpectedly had to work late after a computer failure had resulted in a huge amount of data being lost which needed to be re added. She briefly left at 4.30pm for an early dinner then returned at 5.30 pm just as the staff were leaving, she started work not long afterwards, hoping to be finished by 10pm. At 6pm the night security based in the gatehouse phoned through to inform her the building was now alarmed and to please call when she wished to leave. She had thought she heard a dragging noise not long after this call but paid no attention.

At around 9.45pm Mrs Pritchard was startled to hear footsteps in the corridor outside her office. She stopped typing and listened intently to the slow soft footsteps walking from the canteen end of the corridor, past her office and carrying on towards the laboratories. Every so often the unknown personage stopped and the sound of a door handle being tried could be heard.

As quietly as she could, Mrs Pritchard phoned the gatehouse and asked if anyone else was in the building, after an emphatic "no", Mrs Pritchard started to feel frightened. The unknown visitor went on trying doors, softly wandering along the deserted corridors. After five minutes the intruder's footfall seemed to fade completely.

Mrs Pritchard put her coat on and hurried downstairs, at which point she heard the footsteps again some way off.

"Who's there? I've called security!" she shouted out. In conjunction with this she pushed open a fire door, the intruder alarm sounded and security were on the scene in two minutes.

Mr Haskins, after hearing the story yet again chipped in.

"It was your imagination Mrs Pritchard; I've often worked late in this building and never heard footsteps, and don't forget the alarm was working so it can't have been a burglar."

"I'm telling you the building is haunted, I heard ghostly footsteps, there's a lost soul here. Mr Halfpenny will carry out an investigation and route out the evil."

"This is the last straw! An investigation? Isn't that where lots of people run around in the dark screaming with a camera in their face?" exclaimed Mr Haskins.

The massive frame of Halfpenny shook with a booming laughter, then after wiping his eyes with a crisp white initialled handkerchief politely added,

"No, no Sir that's on television I can assure you. I always have a hefty nosh up before I start a night investigation, so with that and my size I don't reckon on doing much running about."

"Oh" replied Mr Haskins slightly taken back and then after shuffling some papers enquired "What do you do then?"

"Well Sir it's like this, firstly I will ask a few questions to some of your members of staff and find out what I can about the building. Then I will hold a lone vigil in the building at night."

With growing impatience, Mr Haskins raised his eyes to heaven and replied "But what do you actually do?"

"Nothing Sir" was the jovial reply.

Mrs Pritchard, acting as a mediator, hurriedly explained it was the job of Mr Halfpenny to observe and document haunted locations and if warranted based on his evidence sanction a full-scale investigation. Mr Haskins patience was at the end of its resources, he paced the office and then finally after a short pause said,

"I won't allow all this. You invite some Stranger into the company - right at a crucial time and expect me to allow him to walk about on his own in a restricted area. I don't know anything about him. It's like having the Don from a Sandeman port bottle pay a visit." The office once again rattled to the sound of Halfpenny's laughter.

"It's the way you tell them sir and your delivery, you'll be the death of me" joked the big man.

Finally, after negotiations that would put Brexit to shame, it was agreed that paranormal investigator, Theodore Halfpenny, would spend two nights monitoring events at Pritchard and Ross.

In a slight defence of the flustered Mr Haskins, it should be pointed out that the company was going through a crucial period that all hoped would lead to a government contract.

Leonard Pritchard and his Partner Clive Ross started the company in the late 1950's. Its primary product back then was a range of fuel additives that were developed for motor racing, and were still in production today. Since then a relatively new venture had opened up – the testing of car and agricultural tyre compounds. A large downstairs work shop carried out no end of tests on a wide range of tyres, burst tests, rolling resistance, failure analysis and forensics, accelerated aging, etc. The list was endless but all fell within government compliance.

However, the "crucial time" to which Mr Haskins spoke so strenuously of, was the testing and development of a new secret additive which in theory could cut harmful emissions and significantly increase fuel economy in the heavy goods and agricultural vehicle sector. Tests and experiments were ongoing, but it showed great promise and advisors for the Transport Minister were keenly following progress. It was widely believed that Pritchard and Ross were months ahead of their rivals - Mr Haskins was determined to see it stayed that way.

Later that Friday afternoon at around 5pm Theodore Halfpenny once again entered reception clutching a creased leather cricket bag and cordially announced his presence. All that was missing from his arrival was a puff of smoke and a white rabbit. With Mr Haskins out of the way dealing with a haulage company that had failed to collect a selection of farm tyres the night of the ghostly visitor, Halfpenny set about interviewing a few members of staff before they all left to enjoy the Friday sunshine.

He learnt a fair bit more from Mrs Pritchard. Her decision to work late the night in question, was a complete spur of the moment action and one only her and security were privy too. He also found out that all staff had to swipe in and out of the building via a turnstile that was connected to the company computer system. Mrs Pritchard checked the computer programme that controlled this system and found no discrepancies. All staff had left on time on the night in question.

The late afternoon sun streamed cheerfully in through the metal framed windows to such an extent that the great man removed his tent like cape and hung it on the hook alongside his hat. With this garment gone it revealed him to be clad in a dark purple crushed velvet suit with a ruffle white shirt and black string bow tie. The whole outfit gave the impression of a 1970's after dinner speaker. His eyes squinted behind gold pince-nez as he scrutinized the computer screen.

"Very wonderful things these aren't they?" he remarked – but before Mrs Pritchard could offer a reply he spoke again. "What does this black mark against this name mean?"

"Oh, that's poor Mark Webber, one of our senior technicians he went home poorly yesterday at midday. He ' phoned in again this morning still sick. The black mark means absent."

Next, Halfpenny made his way to the staff canteen where he briefly spoke to Mrs White the cook. Ironically, she looked exactly like her namesake in old versions of the board game Cluedo. She had never seen or heard anything mysterious in the building during her 12 years with the company, and could offer little help to his investigations. Instead she launched a harangue about the night security guard Mr Phillips, who had been called to the building the night of the upset to search it.

"Was that not what he was supposed to do then?" gently retorted Halfpenny.

"I dare say, but it didn't give him the right to take two of my lamb pasties and a pint of milk for a snack!"

"Thank you Mrs White I will proceed with all vigour and speak to Mr Phillips now. I trust you pass a peaceful night," and with that the towering Halfpenny headed to the gatehouse.

Mr Phillips was a very agreeable fellow, but like Haskins and Mrs White he had never experienced anything supernatural in the main building. He gave Halfpenny his version of the events of that evening.

"It was just before 10 ten pm, Mrs Pritchard had pushed open a fire door and set off the main alarm. I was with her in two minutes, she seemed quite unnerved and she was adamant that there was someone or something in the building. I searched the whole building Sir, from top to bottom, toilets, canteen, cleaners' cupboards you name it Sir. But when I first climbed the stairs, I thought I heard a scraping noise but couldn't be sure."

Halfpenny scratched underneath his excessive beard nodded slightly and then in a flat deep voiced asked, "All the rooms?"

"All the rooms that I have the code for, - I was over two hours making sure the place was empty. I even had a colleague come and help, and I also carried out random spot checks for the rest of the night in addition to my outside patrols," Mr Phillips replied.

Halfpenny thanked him for his help and in return was wished well with his "ghostbusting" later on.

After a whistle stop tour conducted by Mrs Pritchard, they returned to her office at 5.30pm and she pumped him for information on his findings so far. He looked preposterous sat in a tiny office chair, which any minute looked like collapsing under his stout body.

"Bits and pieces, bits and pieces" was the hearty reply. Mrs Pritchard, as if producing a star witness then said,

"Jane, tell Mr Halfpenny dear, tell him." A young office clerk called Jane recounted her story of hearing a "disembodied voice" at 8am this morning. She and Mrs Pritchard were the only one in the admin block at the time. She went on to explain,

"Mrs Pritchard was on the Phone at the time, it was exactly 8am. I just stepped out the office to get water from the cooler when all of a sudden, I heard a muffled voice from all around me! It was awful, I ran back to get Mrs Pritchard but it had gone by then"

At this time the office door creaked open and Mr Haskins entered with a face like a constipated rat.

"Hello there Mr Hoskins" boomed Halfpenny (Jane sniggered).

"It's Haskins!!" came a fuming reply.

"Oh, my dear chap I'm so sorry, I'm a bit hit and miss with names."

The reason for Haskins increasing bad mood soon came to light as he explained.

"That idiot Phillips was so long messing about last night searching for your ghost that when the lorry arrived at the main gate to collect the tyres the driver couldn't get in! Rather than wait any longer and miss his other collection times he drove off! The order will have to be doubled for Saturday morning now."

Mrs Pritchard explained that every Thursday at 11 pm and Saturday at 9am a lorry arrives to collect tyres which have been tested and drop off fresh ones if ordered. Mr Haskins collected his hat and briefcase, begrudgingly wished them goodnight and stalked out of the room with a disapproving air that was Oscar worthy. Before sending Mrs Pritchard on her way, the genial Halfpenny asked her if the two delivery times of which Haskins spoke where always the same, Thursday 11pm and Saturday 9am. She said it had been that way since the tyre testing contract started 6 years ago.

Halfpenny set up his base camp in main reception, and wasted no time in unpacking equipment to aid his paranormal search: sandwiches, newspaper, hip flask, times crossword and sleeping mask. At 6pm sharp Mr Phillips rang the reception phone and informed Halfpenny that the building was now alarmed and would be triggered if any of the external doors or turnstile were tampered with. Halfpenny thanked him kindly and beseeched him not to enter the building unless he absolutely had to.

A sandwich the size of a breeze block was consumed then a cup of tea and a read of the paper.

The spacious reception was peppered with early evening sunrays, warming and brilliant - some catching lazily floating dust. The scattered leather chairs, large palms and swiss cheese plants reflected in the mirror like floor gave the place an oasis quality and Halfpenny was soon fast asleep. Just before 8pm he awoke from his slumber; the sun was lower in the sky now and the reception was a little gloomy.

"Better make my first observations," he muttered.

The large stair case with metal banisters lay directly in front of him, and he made his way up astonishingly silently, note book in hand. The next level was familiar to him, the stairs brought him out three quarters of the way down a long wide corridor. In front of him was a photocopying room then two doors down Mrs Pritchard's office and next to that Mr Haskins office and anti-room. To his left the corridor went on a considerable distance but was brightly lit with a large window at its end, which also marked the point it veered off to the right leading to the laboratories. To his right the corridor ran another 30 feet or so before coming to an abrupt end and a solid wall, against this stood a large water cooler and a small table with a spider plant on.

Halfpenny's girth caused a total eclipse in the long corridor as he turned left and proceeded towards the window. Some doors had push button access while others didn't, most had names on them, "Network Room, Comms Room, Secure Document Area, and so on. Most doors he noted were locked. He then turned right and another corridor stretched out in front of him for about 35 feet. This corridor was dingy and bereft of windows, 3 doors at intervals were the only adornments. "Lab 1, Lab 2, Lab 3" all were marked with garish authorised personnel only stickers.

He made a few notes in his book using a thick carpenters' pencil which was swamped by his sausage fingers. Just then he heard a soft thud, then an expeditious dragging sound. It definitely emanated from around the corner and perhaps as far back as Mr Haskins office. In perfect corroboration with Mrs Pritchard's experience, he heard the well-placed footsteps and the sounds of door handles being tried, and key pads being punched. He swiftly tried to make his way to the end of the corridor, once there a glance left would reveal the entire length of the corridor and maybe the spectre with it.

As ill luck would have it just outside Lab 2, he dropped the chunky pencil, the sound of it hitting the floor bounced off the walls and seemed as loud as if it had weighed a ton. Just then the phantom footsteps faded away in a brisk scurrying. He turned the corner and anxiously looked. He was met with a perfectly empty corridor... The water cooler and table now looked like dolls furniture viewed from this distance. Nothing stirred at all - no sign of anything living or dead. The owner of the footsteps had vanished into thin air!

Halfpenny arrived back outside Mrs Pritchard's office and made some more notes only stopping his scribbling to take a gargantuan swig from his leather-bound hip flask. He then moved further down the corridor eventually arriving back at the water cooler and table.

"Hmm this is worthy of a note or two," he said. He studied the corridor in more detail and even paced and measured certain areas. Happy that he had rung dry all the information to be gained he walked back to the stairs and once again descended to summarise his findings so far. He logged the time at 8.19 pm.

More libation followed and a brief rest, he glanced across the other end of reception and his eyes met the clocking in turnstile. With no renewal of sound from upstairs he indulged in another large belt from his hip flask and walked over to examine the solid metal bars of the contraption. On the left- hand side was a small grey box with three lights, employees would offer their own personal card up to this, when a green light was displayed, they could then proceed and turn the metal bars one half rotation before they locked again, thus allowing them out and making sure no one could follow and leave undetected. The same procedure followed for entry on the other side.

Keeping the turnstile in view he stepped backwards until he reached the reception desk and stretched out his arm then rested his chin on it and let his eyes make calculations. Not long after these calculations he seated himself at the reception desk, and under the light of a desk lamp soon became glued to his Times crossword, while all the time listening in case the phantom on the next level once again became active...

At exactly 11.48 pm the hulking Halfpenny once again heard the soft thud, which as before heralded the footsteps. He tip-toed over to his cape in a fashion which conveyed a perfect impression of Oliver Hardy.

Now wrapped in the garment he slowly climbed the stairs not making a sound, he had gained the appearance of an ominous granite rock face as he reached the top. Halfpenny then stopped and nestled back into the shadowy corner of the stairwell, he merged with it perfectly thanks to the cape's blackness. He could see the door to the photocopying room and a small portion of corridor. Very slowly the photocopying room door opened and almost at once a mysterious inky figure exited. This appearance then stealthily headed in the direction of the laboratories taking the familiar soft footfalls with it. Every so often the figure stopped and tried a door handle. Halfpenny leaned his head round the stairwell wall and noticed an eerie white light emanating from the appearance, then he heard a faint tapping or stamping noise.

Mrs Pritchard's ghost continued its perambulations for some time. Halfpenny watched in silence and logged everything in his mind, ready to be transferred to notes later on. The visitor came and went several times, up and down the corridor, back to the photocopying room, then back to the laboratories and then that odd tapping noise could be heard.

Finally, the dark figure headed down the corridor which led to a dead end, after a few muffled noises silence returned.

Halfpenny shone a torch on the wall, the water cooler and table were the only things visible, the shadows of these two objects moved and distorted eerily in the torch light. He checked his watch - 27 minutes had elapsed since the visitor first showed itself.

"Hmm, now that's a manifestation and a half," he thought to himself as he leisurely headed back to his base in reception, all the while being careful to not make a sound. Once back at the reception desk, Halfpenny once again swigged from his hip flask and devoured another slab sandwich. Before removing his tiny pince-nez and replacing them with the eye mask, he made copious notes and muttered a few words almost as if formulating a theory. He reclined on the chairs and fell into a restful slumber, confident the "ghost" would not walk again that night.

The snoozing giant woke a little before 6am and immediately scanned his surroundings, then levered himself up from the leather chairs with the finesse of a wrecking ball being pulled from the side of a wall.

Over at the reception desk he produced a well-thumbed address book from his cricket bag and adroitly flicked through and stopped at a name, then picked up the phone and started to pummel the buttons.

Mrs Pritchard answered in alarm, "My dear Theo are

you alright? Has the ghost attacked you? I knew I should have stayed!"

"No, my dear I'm fine but I do need your help contacting a few people" he replied chuckling.

"Contacting! Should I bring my Ouija board?" she proudly exclaimed.

"Good heavens no dear, I think we can manage without that, can you meet me at reception at 7.30 please and I will explain everything", he warmly asked. Beside herself with excitement Mrs Pritchard agreed.

"So, is there a ghost?" she asked before going.

"Oh, there's a presence here my dear, a wondering frustrated figure."

He said goodbye, then called down to Mr Phillips at the gatehouse and told him Mrs Pritchard would be on site in 30 minutes and would he mind unalarming the building for a few minutes so she could let herself into reception, (Mrs Pritchard had her own key to the main doors), he would then call him to re alarm the building straight away.

Exactly on time Mrs Pritchard unlocked the main doors and hurried into reception like a child on Christmas morning, then started calling for Halfpenny.

"Well hello there my dear," boomed the reply from the turnstile. "Be so good as to lock the main door please, thanks awfully," he said in a soothing voice. "I just want to try a quick experiment before phoning Mr Phillips to re alarm the building,"

A minute or so later the building was once again alarmed, with growing impatience Mrs Pritchard asked while tugging his crushed velvet sleeve.

"Tell me everything, Theo spill the beans."

He looked down at her and smiled a knowing grin.

"I will soon my dear but we need to act fast. I need your help in making a few calls and I will also need you to find something for me"

"How dare you call me at home and then demand I come over here on my day off, this pantomime has gone on long enough!" a totally exasperated Mr Haskins barked. The time was now 8.22am and the building once again alarmed after the arrival of Mr Haskins.

"Please don't be cross at Mrs Pritchard, she was acting on my instructions Mr Hodges." Came the cheerful reply from the clouds.

"The name is HASKINS!" came the irate reply.

"Oh, my goodness, I've done it again, you will forgive me?" Halfpenny asked.

Mrs Pritchard acting as mediator again suggested they all go to her office and let Theo explain all. Over cups of tea and a fine selection of biscuits, a volley of questions was fired in quick succession at the paranormal investigator. He remained cheerful and totally unflustered, only stopping his biscuit dunking operations when the supply was exhausted.

Then while in a perpetual pacing, he started to explain. It transpired he found it very implausible from the outset that the building was haunted or "troubled" as he called it. No one up until Thursday night had ever seen or heard anything to suggest such a thing. He also pointed out that spirits tend to be in the habit of drawing attention to themselves not skulking about softly.

"But it was trying the door handles," Mrs Pritchard disappointedly said.

"Ahh yes, it seemed to try every door handle except any that would trigger the main alarm, how very considerate and knowledgeable," he laughed.

Mr Haskins, now in a better mood then asked "So you don't think it's a ghost"?

"Good heavens no Sir, if you'd like to follow me down to your impressive workshop where all those tyres are stacked, I would be happy to show you Mrs Pritchard's ghost."

By the time the caped elephantine had escorted the two down to the workshop and test areas, the roller shutters were just being raised revealing a large flatbed lorry at the loading bay. It was now just before 9am and the routine tyre collection was about to start. Just then Mr Phillips and another security officer appeared and hovered just inside the bay.

"Mr Phillips, who's that with you? I didn't sanction

anymore overtime, why do you need two of you?" asked Mr Haskins in a demanding tone.

Halfpenny politely cut in, "Now sir don't go panicking like an amateur, I asked Mr Phillips colleague to come along."

Now, with all eyes on him Halfpenny resumed his pacing and then after building up his audience he boomed out.

"OK MR WEBBER YOU CAN COME OUT NOW SIR."

His voice echoed around the vastness but nothing happened.

"We are waiting Sir, or should I have Mr Phillips make a search?" Halfpenny continued in a gentler tone.

Slowly one of the colossal tractor tyres stacked on a pallet started to move. Everyone except Halfpenny looked dumbfounded. With the demure of a schoolboy caught cheating at exams, a dishevelled Mark Webber appeared from the tyres and climbed out.

A red-faced Haskins was first to speak.

"Webber what the hell do you think you're doing!? Your supposed to be sick, how long have you been there?"

Halfpenny then calmed the scene, happy with the climax of his stunt.

"Ok Mr Phillips if you and your colleague would like

to take Mr Webber down to the gatehouse and keep an eye on him. Oh, and I had better have those papers hidden down his jumper and those stick things too. I will put my friends in the picture."

Back in Mrs Pritchard's office the beaming investigator answered all questions with a chuckle and polite wave of his shovel-like hand. He first handed the items found on Webber to Mr Haskins. The paper and USB sticks where all "commercial in confidence" and should not have been taken off site or indeed viewed by anyone not directly connected with the new fuel additive formula.

Just then the phone rang and Mr Phillips reported that Webber was, to quote the vulgar saying "spilling his guts". He had been put up to the theft by a rival company in the next county called Timpson & Son.

Finally, after more tea laced with the remainder of his hip flask Halfpenny told the keen audience how he had arrived at his conclusions.

"Mrs Pritchard, your snap decision to work late on Thursday totally scuppered Webbers plan from the word go. Had your decision been common knowledge he could have postponed but it was too late by then, the dye was cast. Having access to 60% of the information Timpson's wanted already, Webber thought his task would be easy. At midday on Thursday he faked sickness and appeared to swipe out and walk home (he lived not far).

"But he did swipe out Theo," came a prostrated call

out from Mrs Pritchard.

"He did, just that, no more, offered his card up to the box and when the green light came on, he stretched his arm through the bars advanced the turnstile one half turn to simulate his leaving."

Halfpenny then explained the turnstile could not be viewed from the receptionist's desk. So, in fact he merely waited until her back was turned and casually walked back upstairs and waited in one of the cubicles in the gent's toilet until lunchtime. At lunchtime with the staff in the canteen he quickly climbed up into the roof space using the table and water cooler as make do step and ladder.

He turned towards Mr Haskins, who by this time was looking mightily impressed, and continued his report.

"I found out from Mrs Pritchard that Webber had laid all the cable for the computers a few years back so he had intimate knowledge of what was above the false ceiling. So, he tucked himself away in the roof space and thought that his plan was going perfectly. All that remained was to wait until the staff left at 5.30pm, for the building to be alarmed and perhaps a bit longer for good measure and then slip down and take the information he needed. But you my dear burst his bubble."

Halfpenny continued, "You remember the dragging noise you heard at just after 6pm? Well, that was Webber - he had dropped down from the false ceiling unbeknown to you and then discovered that some 'helpful' person had moved the water cooler back to its original position thus making climbing back up impossible. "Look over here" he called, striding out the office and along the corridor.

The water cooler was shown to have been moved three feet to the right, directly above the panel Webber used. Making access simple.

"Do go on Theo," Mrs Pritchard eagerly added.

"Webber got such a shock when he noticed through a crack in your door you were at your desk! He didn't dare risk climbing back up, so he waited in the gent's toilet cubicles until you left. By 9.45pm he ventured out again but must have been howling mad to see you still at your desk. With his time running out he decided to proceed with his plan and hope you didn't see or hear anything."

"Good god the tyre collection!" this time it was Mr Haskins who interrupted the lecture.

The all too familiar booming laughter filled the corridor.

"You got it Sir" Halfpenny cheerfully replied.

He then explained he had asked Mrs Pritchard for the plans of the building early that morning, it not only showed a large void above the water cooler, complete with a boarded floor but a narrow walkway 22 feet in length leading to the tyre workshops. It ordinarily would have been too long a drop but there were stacks of tyres underneath making it no more than 5 feet to the first one. He planned to leave the premises with the required formula by hiding in a large tyre and waiting to be collected at

11pm.

"Well we all know how that ended," Mrs Pritchard added ashamedly.

"With his plans in ruins and his means to exfiltrate probably gone, Webber had scurried back up to his hiding place. Mr Phillips searched the building for two hours and also at random times throughout the night making it impossible for Webber to attempt the lengthy search of offices and laboratories. This also explained the loss of Mrs White's Pasties - realising he would be stranded in the roof for the rest of the day he had helped himself to two of them and a pint of milk. I bet the bottle is still up there Sir! His new plan was to stay concealed all day Friday get the information Friday night and then leave via the regular Saturday morning tyre collection. He could not leave via the turnstile or use his card on any swipe access door or it would register his presence. I must admit that after dropping my pencil the night before and hearing the footsteps running away and then seemingly disappear, to having my doubts. But they were quashed when I noticed the water cooler had been moved from the position I had seen it only moments beforehand, and also one of the spider plants leaves had been crushed. Poor Luckless Mr Webber had chosen the moment I was around the corner by the laboratories to jump down from the roof and move the cooler to aid his climb back. No doubt the same well-meaning member of staff had once again put it back in its correct place during the day."

Halfpenny paused to take a breath. Haskins and

Pritchard were both spellbound waiting for the next instalment, they were not to be disappointed.

"Remember the disembodied voice that scared young Jane yesterday morning? It was Mr Webber again causing more unsuspecting mischief. He had to phone in sick at 8am before someone here called his landline and asked if he was going to be absent again - that would have alerted his wife. If you recall Jane was just about by the cooler when the muffled voice was heard. During my vigil I had observed Mr Webber moving back and forth down the corridor, although this time the ghostly illusion was broken, with my suspicions realised, I watched him at leisure. I had taken the added insurance of wearing my rubber soled shoes after hearing the giveaway squeaking my other pair elicited on the shiny floor. He took some papers out of the document room and photocopied them and methodically returned them. He also took some time working out the codes to the doors he didn't normally have access to."

"Impossible!" objected Mr Haskins in a wounded manner. Halfpenny resumed his speech.

"I'm afraid not Sir, the raised metal buttons had all been coated in a UV marker pen sometime earlier. It's totally invisible in normal light and requires a special torch to view it. Now after dozens of the correct code being entered Mr Webber would have a clear pattern of which buttons had been pressed, it was then a matter of running different sequences. He did this for Lab 1 and 2, he knew the combination to 3 already as he worked there. Very sensible of you to compartmentalise people sir, if I may say."

Halfpenny then finished off by telling Mr Haskins he would also find more sensitive material on those fancy memory sticks Webber had about his person.

"The rest you know, he returned to his place of safety to await his lift out the main gate. I did take the precaution of obtaining his home phone number from Mrs Pritchard this morning, and kind Mr Phillips obliged me by phoning his wife on the pretext of routine security checks. He found out that she had not seen her husband on Thursday due to him working late. She had left for her evening cleaning job as per normal at 7pm and she normally returned home at 7am. Just before 7am, she received a text from him saying he had been called into work early to deal with a problem. That explained most of his absence, but I imagine she wants a word with him now more than you Sir," he roared.

"Theo you've done it again," applauded Mrs Pritchard.

Mr Haskins was still mulling over things and after a minute or so asked

"Why on earth didn't he just run out the building with the information rather than hide?"

Halfpenny started packing his cricket bag as he answered Mr Haskins in an amiable manner.

"I think you would have been more than suspicious Sir if the intruder alarms sounded here and Mr Phillips reported seeing someone running away, then a few weeks later your main competitor announced they were as close to the finishing line as your company in this fancy formula."

Making his way to the door he also explained that's why he kept all the alarms on until the last minute, if Webber had had the slightest suspicion the alarms were off, he might have made a break for it.

Webber had had the slightest suspicion the alarms were off, he might have made a break for it.

"Poor devil was trapped, if he had used his card to get out it would have shown, and if he set the alarms off, and a break- in suspected, the information would have been too hot for the other company to handle"

"I can hardly thank you enough Mr Halfpenny, you have literally saved our bacon," swooned Mr Haskins.

"No need to thank me Sir, it was you and Mrs Pritchard's foresight in allowing me to investigate that really saved the day," he winked at the blushing lady.

"Yes, I guess I did have a part to play in allowing Mrs Pritchard to avail us of your services," Haskins announced with a slight wobble of his head.

"If you will both excuse me now, I have to see the vicar in an hour, he has a suspected polkerdise in his bell tower."

"No, no Theo it's Poltergeist," corrected Mrs Pritchard.

The booming laughter disappeared into the radiant morning sun and growing hustle of the warm Saturday.

Clipping from evening post (Wiltshire Edition)

Legendary ghost hunter Theodore Halfpenny uncovers industrial espionage after being called to catch a spook. The Quaker Oat hatted legend wasn't fooled for long, and soon discovered that things that went bump in the night had a much more monetary motive! A member of staff was caught red handed and has since been dismissed. Speaking early today Mr Halfpenny said "I'm very pleased with the outcome and must thank my dear friend Mrs Pritchard and company manager Mr Hastings"

JOURNEY OF ALL OF THE DEAD

Britain's former railways, thousands of arterial miles reaching out across the country. Generations born and bred into its back-breaking tapestry. The huge infrastructure needed to sustain the giant played host to endless memories and event's that have since become ingrained into the very fabric of the buildings themselves.

Early in November Terry Mathews arrived outside his company headquarters to be given details on his new assignment. He was only in his early 30's but already a seasoned veteran of the security industry and in particular night work.

The 'headquarters' in actual fact consisted of an ex police scene of crimes portacabin on a scruffy rundown industrial estate. Many of the units were now boarded up behind chain link fences - the former occupants' endeavours long since liquidated and forgotten.

He buttoned his collar and fastened the company issue, cheap black clip-on tie, then made his way over to the cabin, avoiding broken pallets and traffic cones.

"Come on in mate, won't be a minute," was the informal greeting from his rarely seen boss (and company owner).

Terry moved some box files off a battered sofa chair and waited for his lesser spotted employer to finish a phone call. He couldn't remember the last time he had been here, but that aside he was certainly aware that the place hadn't changed. Two dated sofa chairs closest to the door where masquerading as the 'clients waiting area'. His boss had the large desk in the far-left corner, opposite that was the one belonging to his secretary - come cleaning lady - come wage clerk who he only knew by name and had never actually met in 6 years of working for the company.

Stacks of paper and receipts were precariously darted around the cramped interior and the last vestige of professionalism departed the scene in the form of a coffee machine sporting a hand written note on the back of a brown envelope stating it was 'NOT WOKING'.

After five or six minutes the phone call ended and Terry was given his bosses full attention regarding his new night time posting.

The company had the opportunity to gain a lucrative new contract carrying out night patrols around a large railway siding and station. The site in question had been the subject of ongoing trespassing and vandalism issues. Having recently been acquired by yet another privatised company who intended to make more of it than their predecessors, their first logical step was to eliminate the threat of trespass and theft, which up until now had been prolific.

"Could be a real opportunity mate," Terry's boss announced while staring through wire mesh festooned grimy windows. "I asked you over because your perfect for this job, highly respected too."

Yeah, that or the fact I'm 15 minutes from the sidings and my own site has just closed down Terry thought. What a load of guff.

The new owners of the station and sidings had granted a two-week trial, if all went well a rolling six-month contract would be put into place. It would be a two-man site working 12-hour shifts. Terry would start tomorrow night and do the first shift on his own until a colleague could be made available to join him. Terry's boss emphasized the importance of regular patrols, good note-keeping and smart appearance so as to impress the clients - as they were bound to be keeping an eye out.

Terry took the details from his boss and stole another quick look round the insalubrious cabin.

"Yeah, I agree, we don't want them thinking we are disreputable" he sarcastically replied.

...Terry arrived at his new assignment at 6pm on a bitter night, parked his car as close as possible. He then immediately made his way to the disused station on platform one to meet a representative and to be shown around.

A Mr Steven Blake was already on the unkempt platform pacing about and rubbing his hands together to keep warm. He looked about 19, underneath a hi-visibility vest he was sporting a dreadful shiny grey suit and matching shoes. After a brief introduction, the young man inflicted a wet fish handshake and set about a hastily conducted tour.

The site was roughly six acres and when viewed from the south was laid out thus. On the left there was rail track that branched off quite sharply for a hundred and fifty feet then met with a buffer stop. Set further back from this was a fair-sized engine shed with two large soot stained arched openings at each end. The two facing the ticket office had massive dirty white wooden doors, while the two on the other side had both been bricked up and smaller square doors created. Along each longer side there were three sets of well-proportioned square windows. A diminutive oblong shaped building jutted out in the space between the two doors on the south side. It had a pair of windows side by side, and the roof barely came level with the top of the arched portals. In front of this building stood a much newer looking metal shed of some kind with a sloping roof. The immediate area surrounding both of these structures was strewn with large rubbish heaps and patchy grass.

To the left of the forlorn engine shed there was another rusty rail track directly in line with the station. It came to an end about 30 feet from the building and it too had a buffer stop.

No more than 15 feet to the right of this were the former main line double rail tracks, now choked with weeds, and the ballast beneath them heavily oil stained. The tracks continued on past the abandoned station on Platform One and the featureless platform two on the opposite side. They then curved slightly to the right, at which point a pedestrian bridge spanned them. The arch of the bridge was a heavy iron green lattice while the steps leading up to it on both sides were concrete and dark brick. The bridge more or less marked the end of the area to be patrolled.

A fair way further on past this was a large signal box and a scattering of newer buildings. The area behind and to the right of Platform Two was the most neglected, and a thick layer of scraggy grass had started covering the remains of platform three. This looked longer than the other two and also curved considerably to the left in the direction of the footbridge. Small bushes and endless brambles were also taking up residence at random intervals.

This portion of the sidings had three sections of track in varying states of decrepitude. The first was set back away from the other two - on its rusty rails it played host to old rolling stock in the shape of 5 BR mark 2 carriages all in rundown condition. The second track curved to match that of the platform and seemed recently used - it had a long line of box wagons and aggregate hoppers on it, and these carried on well past the foot bridge.

The third section was the shortest and merged with the second just before the overgrown platform. Its length was almost completely taken up by two large diesel locomotives in tired yellow livery and parked buffer to buffer. Most of the site especially that on the left closest to the town was surrounded by a large red brick wall, easily 10 feet in height, daubed in colourful graffiti at various points.

Eventually the two made their way back to the old empty station. After handing over some keys and a list of contact numbers and informing Terry there was a table and chairs in the waiting room and to make himself comfortable, Mr Blake departed for the night.

The station was a medium sized single-story grey slated building with a chimney stack at each end. It was pale yellow in colour with an ornate but peeling white awning protruding out.

There were three black doors leading out onto the platform. Above each there was a glass arch panel, then around this a darker coloured stone surround with an ornate keystone set in the centre. The first single door on the left hung on one hinge. There were three arched windows between this and the main double doors, then a section of wall before another single door, then another row of three arched sash windows, each having the same darker stone surround with centre keystone and matching sills.

Terry glanced around briefly at his new surroundings then pushed open one of the main double doors and headed inside.

"Christ, no wonder he was waiting for me outside, it's colder in here," he said out loud with some distain. He found himself in a large waiting room or reception, the remains of the ticket office were on his right. Years' worth of dust coated the floors and walls, and in numerous places small parts of the ceiling had fallen down. A jagged dirty recess on the left indicated were a fire place had once stood, and on the right near the ticket office was a rickety trestle table and folding chair already set up.

Make myself comfortable - what a joke, he thought.

Being a seasoned night shift worker Terry always loaded his car with one or two little 'luxuries' to aid his night stints. He wasted no time in leaving the cheerless waiting room to retrieve them.

A thin layer of glistening frost had already begun forming on the windscreen of his car as he collected a large duffle bag and headed back to the station.

"Now if I can just find a socket that works," he said as he looked about under the dim single light. Eventually he found a socket that wasn't cracked, hanging off or vandalised and crossed his fingers - yes it worked. He plugged in a little blow air heater and warmed his hands. Next, he arranged the rest of his kit and decided to have a quick look around the building before heading out. There was little to be seen in the ticket office other than some shelves and old notice boards in one corner as everything else had been removed. The door leading out to the other side revealed another waiting room but smaller than his. The light was broken so he shone his torch around, revealing a large central table with two chunky bench seats next to it.

Before leaving on patrol he cautiously toured the outside of the station making sure all doors and windows were locked. The third door on the right had a faint sign saying 'Parcel Office'. Around the corner from this was the gent's toilet. The door that was delicately hanging on one hinge led into a narrow hall with some sort of kitchen or refreshment room on the left, then a mould infested office and finally more toilets. He secured the door the best he could, then headed off in the direction of the foot bridge.

The frigid air stung his cheeks and watered his eyes as he quickened the pace, his footsteps ringing metallically on the platform, the sound ceasing as he then made his way down an overgrown path until the rusty lattice work of the bridge towered above him. He surveyed it through white torch light then made his way up the stairs.

Once in the middle of the bridge he looked out over the whole of the sidings. Large floodlights on tall posts cast other-worldly orange hues in some areas while others remained pitch dark. Other than the faint hum of traffic in the direction of the town, everything was quiet and eerily still. He descended from the steps on the opposite side and crunched along the side of the track casting an eye over the grimy wagons and hoppers. Carrying on further he passed the station with a faint glow emanating from the arched windows. Terry walked as far as the engine shed, glanced at his watch, nearly eight pm.

"Right that will do for now, time for tea" he said and

headed back to Platform One.

The little heater did help to lift the cold sombre atmosphere in the station, and with the aid of a cushion and blanket, the horrid chair provided, became halfway comfortable.

Throughout the night Terry conducted random regular patrols, it never ceased to amaze him as he went about his watchful duties just how quiet the place was. By midnight a large brilliant moon shone down, the beams mixed with the orange flood lights and velvet frost coating to intensify the bizarre effect.

The whole of the sidings, platforms and buildings had an indefinable something about them, something he couldn't work out, or wanted to. Something which made him glad he would have company for his next shift. The following shift Terry arrived at the station in good time and was greeted with a disembodied voice from somewhere in the building that shouted.

"Hello, who's that?"

"Surely I should be the one saying that?" Terry replied more amused than alarmed.

The booking office door opened accompanied by the reluctant groan of dry rusty hinges, then a young-looking portly man with thick round glasses and poor fitting uniform appeared clutching a torch.

"Hi are you Terry? My name's Mike, Mike Tudor, it's my first shift tonight, I'm new with the company, actually this is my first job with them."

"Hi Mike, nice to meet you - they gave you a real shoddy start with this one," then Terry shook his hand.

"No, I really like it, I've just been looking about, shame so many original features have been stripped out."

Terry gave a little snort, and added - "It loses its appeal at two in the morning believe me."

Mike didn't look at all discouraged. After another glance round he then asked Terry what the engine shed was like inside.

"I'm sorry I have only worked here one night myself mate. I only checked it was locked when I passed it a few times - looks a bit rough though."

Terry unpacked some items and once again plugged in the heater. He asked Mike to bring the bench in from the little waiting room and put it alongside the table.

Over the first cup of tea of the night Terry explained to Mike about the role of the job and some other bits and pieces. He also found himself having to calm the younger man's over enthusiasm.

"What do we do in a physical combat situation with vandals!" Mike asked in a fervent manner.

"Dial three nines and walk away," came the reply.

Still his enthused passion remained only slightly dented. Another barrage of spirited questions was then fired off in salvo and echoed in the empty building.

"Mike, did you see the head office portacabin? Did you see a secretary? I bet you didn't - it's a one-man band, minimum wage setup. Please don't go putting yourself at risk, we are just a deterrent here. If anything happened, you'll be forgotten as quickly as yesterday's chip wrappers."

Mike looked deflated and crestfallen, he nodded and turned away. Terry felt a bit of a grouch.

"Come on mate let's go and look at your engine shed then," he said.

The long line of dirty goods wagons had been shunted away sometime during the day giving the sidings a more baron windswept feel. Other than the weather turning milder and threatening rain all else was the same as the previous night.

Terry tried a large key in a huge black padlock and eventually persuaded it to turn, both of them then swung the massive wooden door back and shone torches inside.

"Did you see that?!" Mike exclaimed.

"See what?"

"I thought I saw something move in the torch light over there by that inspection pit."

The two men warily took a few steps inside the blackness of the shed. The towering brick walls were finished in two tone paintwork, the roof was a complicated mass of metal frames, supports and beams, above these were long narrow skylights. The floor was stained with oil and littered with debris - on the right a large area was taken up by a dilapidated locomotive. Mike informed Terry it was an 08 shunter. Terry walked further inside, making sure to avoid a black viscous oil puddle. The place was cold and unwelcoming to the point of hostile. He flooded the inspection pit with light, it was strewn with rubble and broken metal supports, over by the bricked-up arches there were some cable drums and oil barrels stacked up.

"Nothing here mate," Terry assured him.

"But it looked like someone running from one side to the other."

The two men retreated from the unwelcoming building, locked it and continued on their patrol amid a threatening sky. They checked the whole perimeter, making copious notes on which lights were not working. Then on Mike's behest they stopped to look over the parked locomotives. The mountainous relics gave off a greasy fuel tinted odour in the stiffening breeze.

"Class 37 - used to be lot's about but getting rare now," Mike called out while clambering up the closest one to them and peering into the filthy window. Terry stood to the side of the machine and laughed to himself - it was like being a kid - if you stand in front of trains you always have the feeling they might move.

"Come on let's get back, here comes the rain," Terry instructed.

The clouds soon broke releasing dull torrents of depressing rain. Every so often a gust of wind would whistle across the austere sidings rattling the awning and causing the broken outside door to bang haphazardly. After an hour there was still no let up, the two men chatted and paced about in the waiting room amid the cascade outside.

Water dripped from the roof in places and a bone chilling dampness pervaded the whole interior.

"I know what you're thinking mate," Terry said in a joking manner, raising his voiced slightly to be heard over the continuing downpour streaming off the roof and pounding the platform. "Don't worry we won't be based here if the company gets the contract. They will treat us to an ex building site storage cabin or something."

Mike being new with the company failed to see the funny side and gave an awkward smile.

After a few more minutes, and while in the process of scoffing down a cheese sandwich Mike said:

"I'm sure I saw something move in that engine shed."

"Don't worry about it mate, I don't really want to know anyone who has the Jacobs to hide in that place all by themselves in the dark."

Mike laughed, "You have a point." After another pace around he randomly added.

"These sidings were bombed in the war, you know - my Dad told me ages ago. German planes mistook them for the bigger marshalling yards on the other side of town - lots of people were killed."

He then abruptly stopped as if he had offended someone. With the heater full on, doing its best to dispel the soggy atmosphere, Mike made another cup of tea and they went on waiting for the rain to cease.

Terry, who had become a bit of a pessimistic loner

through working nights came to quite like Mike as one or two more night shifts passed. It made a change not to be lumbered with someone who was intent on spending the whole shift trying to convince him they were ex SAS or went off fighting in foreign parts at the weekend - not to mention how tough they all purported to be.

They soon found themselves on the last shift before their scheduled three-day break. The sidings hadn't grown on Terry since then, he still found them too quiet and shadowy for their own good. Their detailed report on lights not working had so far been treated with no response, as a result the lighting was still far from perfect.

Just before eleven thirty, Mike, who had been restless and taciturn most of the shift went out alone for a patrol taking a radio with him, leaving Terry to stay warm by the heater. Terry reminded him to call if he wanted any help.

Terry glanced round at the waiting room, since his first shift they had commandeered some more chairs and another table, swept the floor and got the light working in the other room. Didn't sound much but it was now a hundred times improved since that first frosty night.

Just then the radio let out a static squawk and Mike urgently called.

"Terry, come in mate, are you there?"

"Yes Mike, what's the problem?"

"There's people or something moving about out here, doesn't look" … the transmission cut off…

"Say again Mike, where are you?"

Static...

"Terry, come in mate, they are heading towards you, do you read me?"

"Who are heading towards me? Say again, over", Terry looked out the window into the darkness and down the dim orange tinted platform.

"I'm behind that big pile of sleepers at the far end. There are shadows or people moving around, did you hear me? They are passing the engine shed now, they are getting closer to you..."

Terry put on his coat quickly and stuck his head round the double doors - the chill was discouraging.

"Mike, I still see nothing, over"

Static...

"Terry get out of the building! it's not a joke."

Terry didn't scare easily, he shone his powerful torch down the platform, there was a freezing fog setting in, the beam didn't reach the engine shed. The radio gave another burst of static.

"Come in Mike, over"

Staying calm, Terry walked on a little further, trying the radio a few more times, no reply came. The silence was unbroken, out of the corner of his eye he caught something move but couldn't make out what, it wasn't easy in the slight fog and subdued lighting.

"Terry come in, let's leave, they are all heading to the

station"

"Mike will you stop talking in riddles, who are?"

"They are very close to you!" Mikes voice sounded hoarse and strained.

Terry was about to radio back when he again caught something in motion about 30 feet from where he was standing.

"Christ, what's that!?" he said in shock.

A black tide was advancing in his direction, slowly enveloping the platform, he caught site of other movements within the terrifying profusion.

In a reflexive action to the oncoming threat Terry jumped down off the platform and ran across the two former main line tracks without looking back. The old line of carriages offered the only hiding place from the entity that now occupied the station.

"Mike, come in Mike, meet me over by the carriages, did you get that?"

After a few seconds Mike replied he was heading there straight away. Terry waited in the darkness still unable to look back.

"Is that you Mike? God you were right, it's at the station now! Quick, climb into the carriage and keep low".

The two men clambered up into the musty interior, keeping the torch pointed at the floor and quietly made their way to the centre of the carriage then gingerly perched on two slashed seats being careful to stay crouched. After getting his breath back and regaining a little composure Terry was the first to glance out at the station...

For a brief moment he felt the whole thing had been a ridiculous illusion but then he glimpsed tenebrous figures coming and going on the platform, fleeting activity but ill defined.

"Is that what you saw while out Mike?"

"Yes, it's awful, they were all around me for a few seconds, then seemed more interested in heading to the station, what the hell are they?"

Terry carried on staring in fixated unease, then finally cleared his throat and answered.

"If you hadn't warned me, I'd be in the middle of that now."

The movements sometimes gave the impression of figures, a pale fleck could resemble a face and sometimes for a second or two, limbs might have been discerned, but the movements were so weird and the rolling darkness made getting a clear image impossible.

Mike tapped Terry softly on his shoulder, "Do you think we are safe in here?"

Terry felt like saying something like, 'how the bloody hell should he know', but sensing the younger man was rightly scared senseless and looking for reassurance replied,

"Yes mate, it's like you said, everything is centred round the station. We have a good view here and we are indoors, so let's just see how this plays out."

After another few seconds the hurriedness on the platform died down and the shapes seem to form a straggly line possibly looking over towards the two men's hideout.

"They have seen us!" Mike whispered in a panic, "it's my fault."

Without turning his stare away from the window Terry replied, "No we are safe here, shhh something else is approaching now."

The latest event also entered the stage from the direction of the run-down engine shed. It was moving steadily in the form of a long bulky column of vapour. It carried on down the tracks and approached the station, but the unidentified black shapes on the platform remained motionless. The column partly overran the station and then came to a gentle stop, obscuring most of the building from the two observers view.

Up until now the whole of this activity was void of any form of sound, but with this new arrival a hurried murmuring and dull thuds as of doors being closed could be heard.

"What do you think that looks like Mike?" Terry asked, still transfixed to the spectacle.

Mike edged forward on the frayed seat and looked left then right, then in disbelief gave the chilling response.

"It's a train and soon it will crash."

Slowly, very slowly the obscure vapour gave more hints of what it once was, and now represented. The outlines and sides of carriages with greyish windows became visible. A darting blackness between the windows indicated movement from inside, then the form once again became indistinct. Further on past the station in the direction of the footbridge, there was a sinister reddish glow which emanated from a huge black bulk, casting a deep orange reflection upon the ballast and rusty tracks.

"It's pulling away now I think," Terry said in a halfway reassuring voice. The dark procession slowly started moving off down the track. Every second or two the blackness seemed to morph into a perfectly clear image revealing a tired locomotive hauling six or seven carriages. Then the image once again became dark vapour. It was almost like being out in a lightning storm, for one brief second everything stands out brilliantly and then is gone. A hissing of steam and clanking of wheels and rods seemed to come and go in the freezing air. The two men watched in silence as the uncanny appearance got further away. Then came a chilling ghostly lament from the spectral locomotives whistle. The two men shivered as the sound pierced the silence around them and filled their heads.

After a few more seconds it had merged with its surroundings and was no more, the station now seemed quiet under a white rising moon. Terry glanced in all directions, after satisfying himself all was now ok, he turned to Mike.

"Right, let's head back to the station while it's gone."

Mike however remained bolt upright with his head slightly angled upwards - it was almost as if he knew a second wave of past history was approaching.

"It's not over yet," he said in a sorrowful voice.

Before Terry could answer or do anything the air started to resonate and a vibrating seemed all around.

The two men cowered in fear as shrieks and explosions split the air, thundering down across the sidings, screaming and shouting came in-between the detonations. They expected any minute to be the next target and suddenly cease to exist in a second. Orange flames could be seen dancing round the carriage walls, the sidings were an inferno full of agonized screams and mangled track. This hellish nightmare seemed to last forever. Was this real or just a phantom like that terrible sinister train? Terry finally raised his head and took the briefest of looks out into the glowing tempest...

The station was almost totally obscured by drifting black smoke. The engine shed was on fire, craters littered the area, all around black shapes similar to those they saw board the recently departed train, were darting about frantically. The terrible screaming and explosions continued on and on.

Terry once again buried his head and covered his ears to block out the wailing torment that surrounded their hiding place. Mike hadn't looked out the window at all since the first explosion had rained down. He remained glued to the floor as if the very devil himself was standing over him.

Eventually the vibration and droning from the sky faded away leaving only the screams to be heard. After another short while the screams also departed, not at once, but gradually as if the volume had slowly been turned down. For a few minutes more, all that could be heard was the sound of flames crackling and licking the side of the engine shed. When the fire also disappeared, the station and sidings were left silently brooding under the frosty moonbeams.

The two shell shocked witnesses staggered out from the safety of the carriage not knowing what to expect and walked stealthily across the tracks. Once on the platform they were relieved but not surprised to see the sidings were just as they had always been. The vision of misery from the station's past which had somehow been replayed in shocking detail, had left no traces.

The little heater chattered away in the waiting room and offered some comfort. They did not venture out for the rest of the night, instead they remained holed up expecting any minute the black forms to return and once again pace the platform.

As the end of the shift approached, their fears slowly faded and thoughts of home lifted the mood. Terry asked Mike what he knew of the night's ordeal. Mike was keen to say his bit and explained what he knew to Terry.

"I only found out yesterday myself, that's the truth. I had gone to the library a few hours before the start of my shift, I wanted something to pass the time in-between patrols here."

Terry interrupted, "Hey thanks, I'm not that bad" he said dryly.

Mike carried on as if oblivious to Terry's joke. "I found a book on local railways and the history of all the lines around here before most of them were got rid of." He paused for a minute as if plucking up courage then continued.

"The book gave a detailed account of when these sidings were bombed during the last war."

"But you already knew that mate, you told me" Terry said almost disappointingly.

"That was all I knew, but the book also said there was a strong local legend that the sidings and this building are haunted. He expected any moment Terry would rebuke him, but he was surprised by his colleague's response.

"They are haunted obviously; we bear living testimony to that! I've worked on lots of lonely sites in my time but have never experienced anything like last night. We didn't imagine it Mike."

Mike felt relieved by the older man's reassurances and then added more to the thickening plot.

"About the train... it was really sad." He stopped and cleared his throat, then continued. "The train had just pulled out of the station as the bombers started hitting the sidings, the people onboard must have thought they had had a lucky escape."

Terry looked at him.

"It crashed? You said that last night, what happened?"

"The planes had hit the tracks further up the line and damaged them badly. The driver and fireman were building up speed for the climb up the hill... The locomotive was derailed and slid down a steep embankment taking the first three carriages with it, the driver, fireman and 22 people were killed."

Mike slumped into a chair and added, "It was the train leaving again, maybe it always has done? Those peoples last journey, over and over again."

A wave of stillness washed over the room and lingered.

Terry then asked, "How many people died in the sidings that night?"

"The book said eight," came the hollow reply.

The two men walked out onto the platform and waited to hand the keys over to Mr Blake. Mike wearily stamped his feet on the frosty concrete and looked over to the engine shed.

"It was the anniversary of the disaster last night, same time and everything mate, according to the book."

"So that's why you were edgy before it all kicked off, do me a favour mate, next time warn me," Terry remarked.

Mike was relieved the ordeal was over, then speculated, "I think the whole site will just return to being as quiet as it always has been."

"Yeah too quiet."

Blake appeared late in another toe-curling suit and asked if all was in order.

"Yeah, nothing to report, would need a bomb to wake anyone around here," Terry replied.

...Terry and Mike's boss did not win the contract for the night patrol of the sidings, not through any fault of theirs I might add.

A representative from the rail operator called unannounced one morning at the company 'headquarters' to discuss the finer points of the new contract only to discover a dishevelled man sleeping on the dirty lino floor. When asked to identify himself he proudly announced that he was the owner of the company. Negotiations ended at that point.

...Terry, who had grown weary of temporary postings set aside his hard-line cynical edge briefly and he and Mike submitted a detailed proposal to the rail company to undertake the security of the site themselves. Terry handpicked several of the more discerning guards he had worked with over the years to provide cover on their days off.

This proposal, I am happy to announce, was accepted and the two men worked the site thoughtfully for many years without incident.

The other security guards could never fathom the reason why on a certain date in November, even at considerable inconvenience to themselves, Terry and Mike would insist they work the shift, even if they were on a well-deserved night off.

Two men become life-long friends to the back drop of a terrible tragedy. At the appointed time, they respectfully retire to their cars and let the bloody events replay over again. A minute's silence is given and a heartfelt prayer asking for the journey of the dead to finally end and the lost souls to find their correct place in eternity.

THE SUFFOLK VISITOR

A lonely old farm, set back from the nearest road as if in hiding. Worked by the same prudent family for a couple of centuries. In more recent times a bizarre night visitor, indirectly or otherwise, cost one man his life. 50 years on and that same visitor once again trespasses on the remoteness. Will history repeat itself?

Hill Top farm sits inside the Suffolk border, in fact the last dozen or so of its 300 acres crosses into Essex. A remote Grade Two listed light pink farm house with a traditional huge four stack twisted brick chimney looked down over a long gravel drive.

One night this desolate homestead and its hardworking occupants, the Parker family and Tony, the trusted Farm Manager, appeared to play host to some very strange visitors...

...At around nine forty-five pm on a muggy September night, Peter Parker and his father Brian were locking up the out-buildings and tending to animals. It had been a long hot day and they were looking forward to heading indoors for a good meal. They were standing outside their huge thatched barn some 150 yards from the main house discussing the events of the day with Tony, their Farm Manager, who also rented a small cottage on the farm.

In the bruised sky something quickly whooshes over the barn, Tony was the first to notice it and comment.

"Hey did you two feel that go over head? Felt just like a big draft hitting me."

Brian was inside the barn when whatever it was overflew the farm and felt nothing, but Peter thought he saw something.

"I thought I could see something shiny but it was

very blurred."

The three then slowly paced about outside the ancient barn for three or four minutes looking up into the dusk. Just then the same thing happened again. It was like an enormous object shooting past overhead but devoid of any sound other than a whoosh, no engines or jet noise just a peculiar swishing.

Brian Parker was the first to comment this time. "I felt it that time boys, what the hell was that? A Hang Glider or something what do you reckon?"

"It was too fast for one of those Dad."

Tony had climbed up onto the roof of a nearby tractor by this time, and was gazing in the direction of a clump of trees at the end of a large ploughed field.

"It landed behind the woods by the junk yard, I'm sure of it, I caught sight of something silver going to ground," he shouted.

Peter also clambered up the tractor and his eyes followed the direction Tony's hand was pointing.

"See the old combine? It went down between that and those pine trees."

Peter looked hard but could see nothing there. He was on the point of getting down off the slippery roof when a slight glow caught his eye.

"It's where you said Tony, look there's a faint glow over there, maybe whatever it is has crashed. Let's go and take a look Tony."

Peter and Tony both hastily climbed down from the tractor roof, the light was fading fast and a feeling of anxiety had now crept in. Before Tony could agree or disagree to Peters request, Brian Parker in a firm but wavering voice tried to head things off.

"Leave it for tonight son, it will be pitch dark soon, why don't we all take a look tomorrow morning early?"

"No Dad people might be hurt; it could be anything."

Brian had been edgy since the object had flown over head the second time. He did his best to persuade his son and Tony to look in the morning but it was no good. Curiosity, heroics, call it what you will, or perhaps just a good old-fashioned desire to help in an emergency had overcome any argument Brian could put forward.

"If you must go then take this please." Brian handed his son his single barrel .410 shotgun. "I was going to bag a few rabbits later; I know it's not a heavy weight but you never know…"

Peter raised his eyes to heaven and took the small shotgun. He then retrieved a battered pair of binoculars from the tractor cab that he suddenly remembered he had left in there after a wave of poaching a month ago.

The two headed off down the gravel drive leaving Brian to tell his daughter in law, Emily, back at the farmhouse, what was going on.

"What's the old man thinking of, giving me this thing?" Peter said. "I think he was spooked by that odd sound it made, must admit it was funny."

Speedily the two made their way over the hard-baked earth towards the rusty old combine harvester. All around it were decaying assortments of equipment, ploughs, diggers and another tractor. Emily jokingly referred to it as the 'elephants' graveyard' and was always asking him to tidy it up. They reached the derelict harvester, and noticed that the glow from whatever it was near the pine trees, had intensified. Tony climbed up onto the rusty machine and looked out over the field towards the black clump.

"I think I can make out two shapes over there Peter. They are in that small clearing."

Peter was already looking at the greenish white glow and clumsily fiddling with the magnification on the binoculars.

"I can see those shapes, they look like small pyramids - so it was two objects that flew over the barn, not just one circling the farm," he exclaimed. The two men edged slightly closer, the trees were lit up by the green glow and a soft whistling could be heard.

...Brian walked up and down the huge farmhouse kitchen, with each stride he grew more concerned and impatient. Peter's wife Emily tried to reassure her father-in-law.

"It will be nothing - stop pacing about and drink your tea." But the old man would have none of it.

"It was the sound it made; I didn't like the sound. I'm going out to see what's keeping them - they were only going to the junk yard." Without waiting for a reply, he flung open the latch door and headed out into the oppressive night air.

..."Let's not go any further Peter, I don't like the look of that glow, suppose it's radioactive or something?"

Peter was not listening, instead he was single-mindedly scanning the green glow through the binoculars.

"God what's that moving?! Get down! Something is walking about over there." He crouched down quickly and motioned Tony to do the same.

Peter, sweating profusely, continued in a shaky voice, "There is a very tall odd-looking person striding backwards and forwards from one of the pyramid shapes to the other."

Tony, against his inner reasoning, held out his hand and asked for the binoculars. He wiped the fogged-up lenses and then set about scanning the clearing in the trees.

"Your right Peter, definitely pyramid looking, what's that glow all about? I can't see any movement; you must have got confused with" ... He hurled the binoculars to the ground and glared in terror at Peter. "It's walking this way; it must be eight feet tall. I said we shouldn't have gone any further, it's walking straight towards us!"

...Brian had opened the gate at the end of the gravel drive and was now walking as fast as he could over the rain starved ground. He could just make out a slight glow from the start of the woods. He was worried that the two men might have gone into the woods searching for whatever had landed.

"I'm a bloody old fool, I should have told the boys straight away instead of trying to get them to leave it. Damn thing's come back!" He quickened his pace while all the time repeating the same words with tears in his eyes.

Peter and Tony had raced back to the hulk of the harvester, almost using it as a fall-back position.

"For Christ sake Peter take a look! It might have gone back to the clearing - did you see how long it's arms were?"

"Shut up will you, I'm looking now, ok".

Peter hurriedly raised the dusty binoculars to his eyes while Tony held his breath.

"Oh no, it's closer, run to the barn it will be here soon!"

The two men ran for their lives over the benign field neither stopping to look back even for a second. In the darkness they almost ran into and knocked old man Brian off his feet.

"Dad what are you doing here? Get moving, something landed over there and it's coming this way!"

"I know son, it's not the first time, give me the gun and then wait for me by the barn, I've a score to settle."

Peter grabbed him by the arm and tried pulling him away.

"Do as I say boy! I've never laid down the law to you or shown you the stick as others of my generation would have, but I'm telling you to leave me be!"

Peter looked into his fathers' eyes and knew he couldn't be reasoned with; he would respect his wishes.

"Good hunting Dad, see you at the barn."

The two younger men quickly covered the rest of the field and reached the gate.

"No Tony, don't close it, Dad will be along soon."

Tony, overwrought and exhausted looked over at the dim green light and then back at Peter.

"Your right mate, and I bet he bores us rigid with a long drawn out story."

...Brian Parker was almost at the rusty harvester when he stopped and checked his shotgun was loaded. He suddenly became aware he was not alone. A terrifyingly tall figure noiselessly appeared from behind the machine.

Brian advanced slowly, he seemed full of hatred and
resentment but not fear. When he was no more than 30 feet
from the visitor, he spoke.

"This is the Parkers land, it has been so for 200 years,
what gives you the right to come here and bother us? Have
you not done enough?"

The visitor was clad in a dull silver garment which
clung to it. It was easily over seven feet in height - but
horribly thin with it. The arms came to within inches of the
ground and the hands sported grotesque fingers. The head
was slightly too large for the body and seemed to loll onto
its square shoulders.

"That's far enough! Get back in that contraption and
go bother someone else!" The visitor started to advance on
old man Parker...

... "Dad's been gone too long; we should have just
dragged him home and been done with it," Peter cried.

Tony felt sick and slightly awkward. The barn was
tremendously humid, he didn't know what to say to Peter,
the situation was a nightmare. Emily then ran into the barn
looking pale white and breathless.

"The police are on their way," she said. Peter turned
to Tony,

"What did Dad mean this wasn't the first time?
You've known him 20 years Tony has he ever mentioned

anything to you?"

Tony was using all his concentration to stop from throwing up, he just about managed a shake of the head. They felt like traitors sitting in the safety of the barn while Brian was out there alone. Peter suddenly sprinted out of the barn and into the house, the other two looked on in bewilderment. He returned with a hunting rifle and said he was going to the junkyard. Tony somehow managed to stop him.

"Don't Peter, he asked us to leave for a reason, you saw that look, he wanted to sort this himself."

"I will give him five more minutes, then I'm going out there, don't try and stop me!"

The three of them paced about in the still air, the only sound to be heard was from the horses at the far end of the barn. The wait might not have been so tormented if they hadn't actually seen what the visitor looked like. Tony slipped out of the barn and cautiously walked a little way down the driveway. Peter smoked furiously and wondered what he would say to the police when they got here. That's a laugh he thought, last time he called them out over a trespassing and poaching issue, it took two days for a spotty kid to arrive in a uniform that was wearing him.

Tony then returned from further down the drive,

"I haven't heard a shot Peter so that's good. No one can creep up on your Dad without him knowing."

"That's true Tony, but let's face it, we are not talking

about someone, a him or her, we are talking about something awful that landed down there, and apparently it's not the first time they or it have called."

...Brian Parker raised his shotgun and aimed for the visitor's chest; it was now very close to him.

"You killed my father, now it's your turn!" he screamed.

The gun gave off a crack, a metallic sound told him he had hit his target but the visitor seemed unharmed but did stop approaching. He reloaded as quickly as he could. At the moment there were movements over by the two strange shapes, and then came a sound he had heard described half a century ago - an awful blend between a whispering and a whistle as if produced by hundreds of mouths at the same time.

... "A shot! Right I'm not waiting any longer! You stay here Emily if the police bother to show, send them down - come on Tony."

Just then dragging footsteps could be heard approaching the barn, the three of them froze for a second. Tony grabbed a spade and waited near the huge door.

"What if it's that thing? It might have got past Brian and made it all the way over here."

"Don't do anything until you're sure, it could be Dad. Emily get over by the hay and stay down."

Peter raised the rifle and very warily looked out from

the open door. He could see nothing. It was even more muggy now, the sky was a dark royal blue, insects swarmed around the large light set in the side of the barn.

"Come out and show yourself, we are armed," shouted Peter.

The dragging footsteps got louder and Peters' Dad appeared looking drained and steadying himself against a wooden fence. Peter called Tony to help, they got him back to the farmhouse and locked the door.

"What happened Dad? Did you shoot it?" asked Peter.

Old man Parker sipped at a whisky and asked if all the doors were locked. Only when fully reassured, did he recount what had happened. Tony kept guard looking through a large mullioned window that commanded the best view down the drive.

"Fifty odd years ago the same thing happened boy," he said in a tired tone.

"I was only 21 or 22 then, it was in the summer but I can't remember when exactly. The same noise flew overhead, and I haven't heard that sound again until tonight."

Brian stopped for a breath and Tony took the opportunity to say all seemed quiet from the field. Brian carried on.

"It landed much further away than tonight, on the opposite side of the field close to those scraggy furs we done away with a few years ago, that same faint glow then started."

Peter wanted to hurry the old man; he was desperate to learn more about this hidden event which had now reoccurred.

"My father was a hard man Peter and was known to have a temper. He wouldn't let me go with him to see what it was, back then you didn't argue. He set off full of curiosity much the same as you two did tonight, a few hours later he was dead."

Emily looked over at her husband in shock then stared into Brian's half-closed eyes and asked him what had happened.

"He returned 20 minutes later a broken man, he looked ten years older, shoulders sagging and his knees were bent. Mother got him into bed and called the doctor. I listened through the gap in the door as he spoke in a half delirium. He mentioned a cone shaped object in the trees that gave a pale green light. Then he became agitated as he described figures moving about in the field as if looking for something or taking samples. He kept saying over and over again about a dreadful whispering noise that seemed all around him."

Emily wiped the perspiration from the old man's brow.

"Leave the questions for tonight Peter – he seems to be getting weaker, and needs to rest."

"There isn't much more to tell Emily," the old man feebly added. "He died of apparent heart failure not long after making it home. The doctor was at his bedside and asked what happened that night, as he kept mumbling about being attacked by something."

Tony alerted the others; the glow had started again but this time white and intense. Emily and Peter joined him at the window, it was almost like full day light in the field.

"I'm going to the barn for a better look," Peter insisted.

"Don't Peter" called Emily, but he had already unbolted the door and was gone.

...Peter stepped into the barn, rifle in hand. The horses seemed on edge and restless. He ran across to the other doors that faced out onto the gravel drive. The white light was clearer to him now, and the pyramid shape could still be seen but it was moving into the air slowly.

The great old barn was muggy, an odd sensation seemed to flood it. He turned around quickly but all was still. He suddenly thought what if the visitor has been here while they had been busy looking after his father. He looked around and searched in a panic, but all appeared as it was before they fled into the house. Just then Tony came running in.

"I thought you might need help," he panted.

"I'm sure it's been in here, the place seems odd and the horses are on edge, unless it's because that craft thing is on the move."

"It's what?!"

Tony went over to the door, the shape was now well clear of the tree line, he called Peter and they ventured out. They were just in time to see the second craft leave the ground and rendezvous with the other at the same height. Tony was anxious to get back inside the farmhouse.

"What if they fly straight over us, sounds ridiculous but don't things like this just beam you up?" he said.

A dim row of blue lights could now be seen from each craft, they seemed almost hypnotic.

"They are leaving Tony – look," Peter replied.

The two craft then seemed to ripple - as if looking at them in a reflection - then the glow faded. Without a sound from either they both darted straight up into the night sky, and then stopped.

"Must be easily 1000 feet, what do you think Peter?"

"Hey look they are disappearing."

Again, in total silence the two pyramid appearances uncannily faded away like two unfathomable mirages.

While a doctor tended to old man Parker, Tony and Peter searched the barn but found nothing, eventually the police did arrive and were left speechless when given the complete story, including the newly discovered opening to the whole saga. The ground and area where the things landed seemed well trodden, with two large sections of earth flattened. No other clues to the visitors having ever been there were forthcoming. The little shot gun which old man Parker dropped not long after firing was never found.

It was a mistake telling the Police, as before long, a media frenzy was in full swing and the Parkers had their hands full keeping people away from the 'landing site'.

...Brian Parker made a very slow recovery but his interest in the farm rapidly tailed off and he gained the impression of a man marking time.

Three weeks after the visitor had roamed the land on that clingy humid night Peter returned home to find a large bundle of notes on the kitchen table. He had been away the whole day collecting animal feed and looking over a new tractor.

"What's this money love? Please don't tell me you have given an interview to the press?"

Emily, shook her head and walked over, looking pleased with herself.

"Nope, although I did have a caller today. It was one of those door to door scrap merchant types. They took everything from the junkyard without a fuss! Even had the lorries with them to take it straight away."

"There must be five grand here or more, it wasn't worth half that," he said staring out at the empty area, now with only weeds and tall grass to show where the relics had been.

"They were very thorough, took all the litter too."

Peter furrowed his brow and asked what they looked like.

"I think they were trying to make a good impression rather than looking shabby like that other lot who called a year or two back. There were two, one did the talking while the other stood in the back ground. They both had crisp dark suits and those clip-on tie things."

Peter asked Emily to carry on while they both walked out down the gravel drive.

"No sooner had we agreed a price than the quiet one made a call and all the lorries with lifting equipment arrived. Oh, and I hope you don't mind they also collected some firewood."

Standing at the five-bar gate Peter looked out over the field. A small portion of the pine trees had been neatly felled, no sign of branches or any of the foliage was evident. Looking at the area where the huge old combine had once stood revealed the ground around it had been finely raked over.

"You're not cross, are you? We could do with the money and it saves you and Tony having to deal with it. I thought I was doing the right thing especially after all that's happened."

Peter kept his theory to himself and turned to his wife.

"No, I'm not cross, it was only old junk, I'm sure they will be of far more interest to the people that took them than to us."

A visitor from another world? A military experiment run amok? Why did the mysterious caller return to the scene of its previous landing? How far would you go to protect your property if this happened to you? Maybe the visitor's identity is locked away in the aloof mind of Brian Parker as he stares out over that same field and marks time.

ABOUT THE AUTHOR

My name is Drew Jones and enjoy writing about mysterious and strange events. Some of my ideas are derived from my interest in classic cars, military airfields and the paranormal. I normally write in my study in Wales with my Labrador dog Monty at my feet, and many ideas and plots are thought through on our walks together in the woods. There are lots of ideas buzzing in my head, many involving our sleuth Theodore Halfpenny, who will appear in Mysterious and Strange Events Volume 2 - which I hope to start work on soon!

I have really had fun putting this collection together – so I hope you have enjoyed them too. Perhaps you have read them on your commute to work, on a plane as you travel towards your holiday, or as a quick read at the end of a long day.

As with all authors, I would be grateful if you would leave a review on Amazon – it only takes a second, and is always much appreciated.

It would be very nice to hear from all my readers, so if you would like to contact me personally, please email at:

Andrewjones888@btinternet.com

Printed in Great Britain
by Amazon